"You're the photographer, right?" Reginald London asked.

"Yes," Carrie said.

"That's quite a scream you have," he noted.

"Well, I try not to do it often," Carrie replied with a weak smile.

"Hmmmmm," Reginald said, narrowing his eyes at Carrie. "Right scream, right look, right build, could be perfect-amundo."

"Excuse me?" Carrie asked.

"What's your name?" Reginald asked.

"Carrie Alden," Carrie replied, completely confused.

"Well, Carrie Alden, this just might be your lucky day!" the director said with a grin.

"I'm really not following you," Carrie admitted.

"I mean, Carrie Alden," Reginald said portentously, "how would you like to be in a movie?"

The SUNSET ISLAND series
by Cherie Bennett

Sunset Island
Sunset Kiss
Sunset Dreams
Sunset Farewell
Sunset Reunion
Sunset Secrets
Sunset Heat
Sunset Promises
Sunset Scandal
Sunset Whispers
Sunset Paradise
Sunset Surf
Sunset Deceptions
Sunset on the Road
Sunset Embrace

Sunset Wishes
Sunset Touch
Sunset Wedding
Sunset Glitter
Sunset Stranger
Sunset Heart
Sunset Revenge
Sunset Sensation
Sunset Magic
Sunset Illusions
Sunset Fire
Sunset Fantasy
Sunset Passion
Sunset Love

The CLUB SUNSET ISLAND series
by Cherie Bennett

Too Many Boys!
Dixie's First Kiss
Tori's Crush

Also created by Cherie Bennett

Sunset After Dark
Sunset After Midnight
Sunset After Hours

Sunset Wishes

CHERIE BENNETT

Sunset™ Island

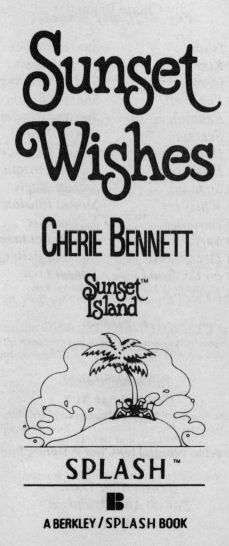

SPLASH™

B

A BERKLEY / SPLASH BOOK

For Jeff, per usual

ONE

"I want iced tea and I want it now!" Samantha Bridges shouted to no one in particular, her wild red hair shaking as she spoke.

"Sam!" Carrie Alden admonished. She and Emma Cresswell buried their heads in their hands in embarrassment at their best friend's demand.

Most of the other patrons of the nearly full Play Café turned to look at Sam. Carrie watched Sam give them a playful nonchalant wave.

"You can't expect to get served ahead

1

of everyone else," Emma said to Sam, who was impatiently drumming her fingers on the table. As usual, the girls sat at their corner spot under one of the Play Café's many video monitors.

"I'm thirsty," Sam opined. "We're here all the time, and we're the hottest babes in here now. So why should I wait?"

"Because there are other customers, too," Carrie said as she reached for her own glass of iced tea.

"What difference does that make?" Sam retorted, her face a study in innocence.

"You just do this sort of thing to embarrass us," Emma said primly.

"*Moi?*" Sam asked innocently.

Carrie rolled her eyes, and Sam cracked up.

"I wish they'd turn up the air-conditioning," Emma said softly, pulling the neckline of her T-shirt away from her neck. "It has to be eighty-five degrees in here."

"Not that it shows on you, ice princess," Sam cracked.

Carrie rolled her eyes again.

"Who's the one demandin' the iced tea?" boomed a male voice.

The girls swiveled in their seats to find one of the cooks blocking the swinging doors to the kitchen. He was at least six feet four, was covered in sweat, and didn't look happy. An angry scar ran from his ear down to his mouth, and Carrie could tell that scar wasn't just an old football injury.

Uh-oh, Carrie thought. *Sam's in for it this time.*

"I said, who's the one demandin' the iced tea?" the cook yelled, striding across the room.

The café was so quiet you could actually hear the music on the rock video monitor. Carrie noticed that the song playing was "Bad Reputation," an old song by Joan Jett. She also noticed that everybody in the place was staring at Sam.

Sam never missed a beat.

"She did," Sam said, pointing a finger directly at Emma. "The hussy."

"Sam!" Emma yelped. "How could you—"

"Lissen up, sweetheart!" the cook yelled at Emma, his face turning an angry red. "I don't want my waitresses losin' time 'cause of you, blondie! What, you think you're special or somethin'? You wait your turn!"

"But—" Emma began to protest feebly.

The cook waved a hand of disgust in her direction, then turned and marched back toward the kitchen.

"I'll get you for this!" Emma hissed to Sam.

"To know me is to love me," Sam said with a grin.

"I mean it, blondie!" the cook yelled back to Emma at the door to his kitchen. "I'm only tellin' youse once!"

"Yes, sir!" Emma called to the cook.

He gave Emma one last withering look, and then went back into the kitchen. When he had disappeared, the entire crowd broke into applause. Sam stood up, clenched her hands over her head like a victorious boxer, and chortled gleefully.

Even Emma was smiling at the prank Sam had just pulled.

That's amazing, Carrie marveled. *Sometimes I think Sam can get away with anything. And look at Emma. I don't know that I would have taken it so well. It's actually kind of funny—Emma is so well bred that she would sooner pull out her fingernails than pull the prank she just took the blame for. Just goes to show that we're really good friends. Great friends, really.*

A day didn't go by when Carrie didn't marvel at the combination of events that had brought her, Sam and Emma together. They had met more than a year before— was it that long already?—at the International Au Pair Convention in New York City. And even though they were totally different from one another—Sam was a tall outrageous redhead from a tiny town in Kansas, and Emma was heiress to the incredible Cresswell fortune—*the* Boston Cresswells—they had all immediately become friends.

Carrie looked over at her two friends and smiled. *And here I am,* she thought, *your basic upper-middle-class girl-next-door from New Jersey, hanging out with these two outrageous girls! Life sure is strange.*

Carrie reminisced about the three incredible things that had happened that had brought them all together. First, they all ended up getting au pair jobs on fabulous Sunset Island, the famous summer resort island off the coast of Maine.

Second, the family that hired Carrie turned out to be none other than rock and roll legend Graham Perry Templeton, his wife Claudia, and their two kids, thirteen-year-old Ian and five-year-old Chloe. Not only was Carrie working at an unbelievable location, but she had employers that any au pair would kill for.

The last incredible thing: Carrie had spent her freshman year at Yale. Emma was at school at Goucher College. And Sam had started at Kansas State University on a dance scholarship but dropped out to dance at Disney World until she found out that wasn't for her, either. And then, they had all come back to the island for their second summer in a row!

We're all so different, Carrie thought. *That's what gets me. Sam is so wild and outrageous and willing to try anything. I'm so average—okay, I'm a good student and take good photographs and Sam wishes she had my curves. And Emma is so cultured and worldly and looks like a princess. Just goes to show that—*

"Hi there," a pleasant female voice with a trace of a downeast Maine accent interrupted Carrie's reverie. "Hot enough for you?"

Carrie looked up. It was Darcy Laken, a tall, athletic girl with gorgeous long dark hair and startling violet eyes. Carrie and her friends had befriended Darcy earlier that summer. Darcy was really nice, really direct, and a little bit psychic. Carrie liked her a lot. With Darcy was Molly Mason, a sixteen-year-old girl who'd been badly injured in a car wreck and now was in a wheelchair. Darcy and Molly lived with Molly's parents in a spooky house up on the biggest hill on the island.

"Hi, Darcy," Carrie said. "Hi, Molly."

"Hey, girlfriends," Sam greeted them. "What brings you out on the hottest night of the summer?"

Molly maneuvered her wheelchair up to the table, and Darcy grabbed a nearby chair and sat down on it backward.

"Oh, nothing," Darcy said nonchalantly. "Except Molly wanted to tell you the news."

"News?" Carrie queried, curious.

"Uh-huh." Molly grinned, her eyes glinting mischievously.

"Don't tell me," Sam cracked. "Howie

Lawrence asked you to marry him and you said yes." The girls all laughed. Howie Lawrence was a really nice but slightly nerdy guy—*hey, it's not his fault,* Carrie thought—who had a big crush on Molly and who had taken her out several times of late.

"Not exactly," Molly said shyly. "Better than that."

"Better than that?" Emma repeated.

"You're having his love child," Sam announced, picking up Carrie's glass of iced tea. "A toast! To the proud parents of—"

"Sam, shut up," Darcy said mildly. Sam put her glass down and was quiet.

"So?" Carrie asked, looking at Molly.

"Well," Molly said, gathering her breath. "My parents' new movie starts shooting the day after tomorrow and it's going to be done right here on Sunset Island and I think we'll all get to be in it," she spilled out without stopping.

"You're kidding," Sam said.

"Nope," Molly replied.

Wow, Carrie thought. *I know the Masons are screenwriters and they write horror films, but I had no idea that they had a movie about to go into production.*

"How come we're just finding out about this now?" Sam demanded. "I could have had my agent send in my picture and résumé!"

"You don't have an agent," Emma reminded Sam.

"So I'll get one," Sam said airily. "Don't bother me with details."

"Well, it's very strange, but my parents are superstitious," Molly explained. "They think if they talk about it, then it might not happen. But Westwood Studios green-lighted the picture—"

"What's that?" Sam interrupted.

"Green-lighted," Molly repeated. "Said they'd actually do it. Said go ahead and shoot the picture. So they start shooting the day after tomorrow."

"Bigger news than Howie Lawrence,

right?" Darcy said mildly, motioning to Patsi the waitress to bring her a Coke.

"And how!" Sam yelped.

"What's the movie called?" Emma asked.

Molly laughed. "Are you sure you're ready for this?"

"Go ahead," Darcy urged her. "They won't hold it against you. You didn't name it."

"*Sunset Beach Slaughter*," Molly intoned.

"My kind of movie," Sam cracked. "Comes with its own barf bag."

Carrie chuckled. *It's one of those slice-and-dice teen films, I guess. Well, this'll be interesting.*

"Maybe it'll have some artistic merit," Emma ventured.

"Maybe Diana De Witt will become a nun," Sam joked, making fun of the girls' archenemy on the island. "But look, who cares if it's art, it's a movie, right? And as everyone knows, I'm supposed to become a movie star!"

"Everyone knows that?" Darcy asked

11

Sam, an amused look on her face.

"Well, only the people I've had a chance to tell," Sam amended.

"What's the movie about?" Carrie asked. An idea was starting to form in her mind. *Hmmm . . . if they're shooting this film here, there are going to be all sorts of show-biz types around. What if I could do a photo essay on the making of a teen horror movie?*

Darcy laughed loudly. "It's a hoot," she said. "It's set right here on Sunset Island. There's this cook guy at a place just like the Play Café—but in the movie it's got a horror theme and it's called the Slay Café. The cook basically goes beserk because all the waitresses and the other kids at the café make fun of him because he got scarred in a kitchen accident—"

Sam cracked up. "Hey, I think we just met him, he's back in the kitchen right now!"

"So anyway," Darcy continued, "he starts killing teenage girls anywhere he can find

12

them. In town, on the beach, at the Slay Café—"

"I think I get the idea," Emma said with a soft laugh.

"My parents are hoping it will out-bloody their last effort—*Massacre at Monmouth High*," Molly said, shaking her head ruefully.

"Gee, I missed that one," Carrie said with a straight face.

Molly shrugged good-naturedly. "Anyway, being in one of these things is hilarious. I had a bit part in one before the Big A."

Everyone knew she meant the Big Accident, where the former dare-anything-once Molly Mason (known as Maniac Mason to her friends) had been left paralyzed from the waist down.

"There'll be a lot of crowd scenes on the beach," Molly continued. "My dad says we can all be in them."

"Great! Fantastic! Excellent!" Sam yelled joyously.

Oh, no. If I know Sam, she's going to think this will be her big break into the movies—how she's going to become a star, Carrie thought.

"Who's the director?" Emma queried.

"Some young guy just out of film school," Molly said. "His name is Reginald London the Third. The studio's very high on him."

"And here's a news flash—the studio is run by Reginald London Jr.," Darcy said dryly.

"How do I get this Reginald London the Third my picture?" Sam demanded.

"Sam," Emma remonstrated with her friend. "The casting for this film is already done. They're not going to put you in it."

"I know that," Sam said proudly, but Carrie could see that Sam actually had no idea how the movie business worked. Emma, Carrie was sure, knew a thing or two about it. She was a film buff who could understand most European movies without

14

subtitles, and she had met a lot of stars in her nineteen years.

"What studio did you say it was, Molly?" Carrie asked mildly.

"Westwood," Molly repeated.

Carrie nodded. The idea that had formed in her mind earlier about doing a photo shoot of the shooting of *Sunset Beach Slaughter* was gelling in her mind.

Now, Carrie thought, *all I have to do is figure out how to get it done.*

"Listen, you guys," Sam said, putting one foot underneath her to sit up higher. "I don't care if they've cast this movie already. This could be It for me!"

"It?" Molly asked.

"My big break!" Sam explained with excitment.

"Make sure it's not the chef who discovers you," Darcy said dryly.

"Let him try," Sam said. "Let him try."

Carrie looked over at the clock on her desk: 1:35 A.M. She sighed and turned over on her back, staring up at the ceiling, feeling tired but really good.

Look at what I just accomplished, she thought to herself. *I came home from the Play Café, called directory assistance in Los Angeles, and got the number for Westwood Studios. Then I called that number and convinced some night guard to give me Reginald London, Jr.'s office fax number. Okay, I lied and told him I had to send him an important fax from Singapore about the foreign rights to* Sunset Beach Slaughter. *So sue me.*

Now all I have to do is write London a letter to convince him to let me do my photo essay.

Carrie was too excited to sleep. She jumped out of bed and put a sheet of typing paper in her portable electric. *Too bad I can't use the computer and the laser printer downstairs. But they're being serviced, and there's no time to wait.*

She stared at the blank sheet of paper. And then it hit her how absurd her whole idea was. *Oh, great,* she thought. *Who do I think I am? I'm going to fax a letter to the head of one of the biggest studios in Hollywood to let me, not yet a sophomore in college, do a photo essay on one of his movies? Yeah, right.*

"You are not talking yourself out of this," Carrie said out loud. She forced herself to begin writing a letter to Reginald London, Jr. She wrote about her background as a photographer, what her goals were, and why she thought it would be good to have a teen take pictures about a teen movie. *Nothing ventured, nothing gained,* she told herself as she finished the letter, took it out of the typewriter, and signed it.

Carrie padded downstairs to the Templetons' office, where there was a fax machine. She faxed her letter and a copy of an article in *Rock On!* magazine that contained some pictures she'd taken.

Faxes don't copy photos well, she remembered as her material ran through the machine. *Oh, well. I have to try. It probably won't work, anyway.*

Finally Carrie was done. She looked at the clock again: 2:30 A.M.

I'm gonna be beat tomorrow, she thought. But she drifted off to sleep with the feeling that she had done the right thing, even if she only had one chance in a hundred of success.

"Oh, who cares?" Carrie said out loud as she snuggled back under the covers. "Like Sam always says, attitude is everything. They'd be lucky to get me!"

She punched a place for her head in the pillow and burrowed in for the night.

Then she crossed her fingers for luck, just in case attitude alone didn't work.

TWO

Bam-bam-bam!

Carrie awoke the next morning to the sound of pounding on her bedroom door.

"Get up, Carrie!" Ian yelled into the room. "You're late!"

"Huh?" Carrie responded groggily, rubbing her eyes.

Ian opened the door and stuck his head into her room. "Breakfast was at seven-thirty today, remember?" Ian reminded her. "I've got the big soccer game against Camp Kohut."

Carrie foggily remembered something

that Claudia had said the morning before, about how a bunch of kids from the club were going to be playing soccer against one of the many summer camps on the mainland.

"Yeah, I'll be right there," Carrie mumbled foggily.

"Well, read this while you're getting dressed!" Ian suggested. He threw the latest issue of the Sunset Island *Breakers,* the weekly newspaper, across the room. It landed at the foot of Carrie's bed. "We're all gonna be famous!"

Carrie, too sleepy to even be annoyed by Ian opening her door without her permission, took the newspaper and scanned the headline. There on the front page, in the island gossip column, the first item was all about the movie.

LIGHTS, CAMERA, BLOOD!
by Kristy Powell
Never mind that the director, Reginald London III, probably got the

gig because he's the son of the studio head. Never mind that according to an advance copy of the script read by this reporter, the Atlantic Ocean is going to run red with blood. Never mind that the film is probably never going to win an Oscar. *Sunset Island Slaughter* starts shooting in two days right here on the island.

The glitz! The glamour! The gore! And this reporter hears that a certain major teen TV star has been secretly cast in the lead. So does that mean that D.D.W. and S.B. are going to be clamoring for his heart? And what will the bass player of Flirting with Danger think?

P.S. A certain BIG rock star reportedly has placed a cut or two on the soundtrack. Stay tuned, dear readers, for lights, camera, and a lot of action!

Carrie whistled softly when she finished the article. Kristy was obviously referring to the rivalry between Sam and Diana De Witt, which seemed to erupt whenever there was anything at all to erupt over.

But I think Sam learned her lesson out on tour with the Flirts, when she went completely gaga over Johnny Angel and nearly ended up busting up the band, and her romance with Presley Travis, the bass player, Carrie thought. *At least I hope she learned her lesson!*

Realizing she didn't even have time to shower, Carrie washed and quickly threw on a Yale sweatsuit. She hustled downstairs to the breakfast table, where the entire Templeton family—rock star Graham, his wife, Claudia (a former secretary at Polimar Records), Ian, and little Chloe—was engaged in a heated discussion.

"You can do it, Dad," Ian was remonstrating with his father between bites of an English muffin. "I know you can do it."

"Morning, Carrie," Claudia said as Carrie slid into her seat. "You're late."

"Sorry," Carrie said, truly contrite. She took her job seriously and hated to be anything less than great at it at all times.

"Okay, just don't make a habit of it," Graham said easily. "We heard how late you got in."

"Sorry," Carrie repeated, sipping her orange juice. *So I was out late, big deal,* Carrie thought to herself. *It isn't like Claudia and Graham to overreact. Well, I'll just have to watch it.*

"So?" Ian demanded, staring imploringly at his father. "Will you do it or not?"

Graham sighed. "It's not that simple, son," he said, sipping his coffee.

"Yes, it is!" Ian insisted. "You're the big star; you just tell them they can't use your song in the movie unless they use one of ours!"

Graham sat back, exasperated. "It just doesn't work like that!"

"But, Dad—!"

"But, nothing—" Graham started to say.

"Why don't you just explain to Ian how it does work?" Claudia said reasonably. "He'll understand."

Graham sighed. "Okay. The thing is, I don't have control. I didn't write 'Cut to the Quick,' the song they're going to use. The songwriters—Victoria Shaw and Gary Burr—have a publishing company who said the songs could be in the movie, and Polimar controls my recording of the tune."

"But that's not fair!" Ian cried.

"That's the way it is," Graham explained.

"Well," Ian said slowly, a glint coming into his eyes, "you may not control the songs, but you still have some influence, right?"

"Where are you heading, Ian?" Claudia asked warily.

"Well," Ian continued, "if the Zits write a song that's tailor-made for the movie, you could pitch it, right?"

"I suppose that's possible, but—"

"Oh, thank-you-thank-you-thank-you!" Ian yelled, jumping up from his place at the breakfast table and throwing his arms around his father. "You're the greatest. Did you hear that, Carrie? The Zits are going to have a song in the new horror movie!"

"Uh-huh," Carrie said as noncommittally as possible, since it didn't seem to her that that's what Graham had said at all.

"Ian," Graham began, "I didn't promise that your song would be—"

"I'll go call the kids in the band and tell them to come over at three," Ian interrupted, and he rushed over to the kitchen phone.

"But what about your soccer game?" Claudia asked.

"We'll be back on the island by two-thirty," Ian explained.

"Carrie, can you chaperone band practice?" Claudia asked. Carrie knew that Claudia was just being polite and that

25

her question was basically an order.

"Sure," Carrie agreed with a grin. "Maybe I'll have some lyrical ideas to contribute."

"Hey, you wrote a song for the Flirts," Graham reminded her.

That was true. Flirting with Danger—or the Flirts, as they were commonly known to their fans—was a hot up-and-coming rock band, and Carrie's boyfriend, Billy Sampson, was the lead singer. Sam and Emma were backup singers, and the whole band had recently gone on tour together. Carrie had gone along as photographer— and had ended up singing with the band for a while! When she and Billy had had a fight, she'd written a song about it, and Emma had sung it as her first solo number with the band.

"That's true," Carrie agreed, "but somehow, writing a love ballad and writing music for a horror movie seem worlds apart."

"You can do it," Graham teased her. "Just make sure instead of using a line

26

like 'making love,' you write, say, 'dripping blood.' "

"Oh, charming," Carrie said with a laugh. "I'm truly inspired."

"Me, too!" Ian yelled from across the room.

"That's exactly what I'm afraid of," Graham said under his breath.

Claudia kicked her husband under the table.

Carrie glanced over at Ian, but fortunately he hadn't overheard his father. As Carrie sipped her orange juice, she thought for maybe the hundredth time how incredibly tough it must be for Ian to live in his father's musical shadow.

Ian assembled the male members of his band, Lord Whitehead and the Zit People, in a semicircle out by the backyard pool, while Carrie sat a discreet distance away. It was that same afternoon, and Ian did not seem at all fazed by the fact that his soccer team had lost to Camp Kohut by the score of 9–0 earlier that day. Carrie had watched the match—*if you could call it that!*—and it was not at all pretty.

"Where's Becky and Allie?" Donald Zuckerman, who played the microwave for the Zits, asked.

The Zit People specialized in something called industrial music, which as near as Carrie could tell consisted of banging on the innards of old appliances with iron pipes. Recently the kids that Sam took care of, Becky and Allie Jacobs, had joined the Zit People as backup singers.

"You are dead meat if you didn't tell them about this band practice," Marc Woods warned, biting a hangnail.

"They're off with Sam in Portland," Ian reported. "They said start without them and they might show up later."

"Oh, real great attitude," Donald sniffed.

"Hey, they're scoping out new stage costumes," Ian chided him. "Anyway, we're the ones with the creative brilliance."

"Yeah, creative brilliance," Marc repeated gravely. "That's right."

Carrie, who was hiding behind a copy of *Rock On!* magazine, barely stifled a giggle.

"So the thing is," Ian said, "we need to come up with a lyrical hook."

"What's that?" Donald asked.

Ian rolled his eyes. "It means the part of the lyric that people are going to remember!"

"How can we come up with a hook when we don't even know what the song is about?" Marc demanded.

William Kerry, the fourth core member of the Zits, rolled his eyes heavenward.

"Yeah, and we also don't know what the movie is about," Donald added reasonably.

"Please," Ian said, a little irritated. "Don't bother me with details. We're talking horror movie, here. So let's do something with a killer theme. Murder, maybe." He reached down and picked up a yellow legal pad and a pencil.

"Someone gets murdered in this movie, right?" Donald ventured.

Ian shot him a bored look. "Have you ever seen a horror movie where someone didn't buy it?"

"I guess not," Donald agreed.

"Okay, you guys, how about this?" Marc suggested:

"He came in the night—
His face was such a fright—
And when the deed was over,
He was feeling quite all right!"

Carrie choked back a huge laugh. Ian looked at her closely.

"Frog in my throat," Carrie explained.

Ian nodded, not entirely believing her.

"That's a start," he said, turning back to the band. "But how about something reflecting the relentless pressure he feels from an unfeeling postindustrial world?"

"Who?" Donald asked, confused.

"The murderer!" Ian yelled with exasperation. An idea flitted across his face. "Hold the phone, hold the phone!" he murmured. He picked up the legal pad and scribbled on it quickly, nodding to himself as he wrote. Marc got bored and sat down to read a comic book. The other two guys thumb-wrestled.

"Okay! I've got it!" Ian finally cried. He read what he'd written on the legal pad:

> "He really felt the pressure,
>   it took him by the hand.
> He really tried to fight it,
>   he didn't understand.
> And finally it beat him,
>   it undermined his life.
> He felt the only answer was
>   to kill 'em with a knife!"

Carrie choked again.

Ian turned to her, his hands on his hips. "Excuse me, Carrie. Maybe you're just too unevolved to appreciate art."

"Maybe," Carrie agreed.

Ian turned to his band. "Well?"

"It's okay," Marc said with a shrug.

"Well, what if the guy in the movie doesn't use a knife?" Donald asked. "What if he uses a power mower or a hatchet, or what if he's like Freddy Krueger and has really, really long fingernails—"

"So we adapt the lyric, then!" Ian interrupted. "This will just show them what we can do, right?"

"Well, I guess so," Donald said. "But, like, *lawn mower* or *hatchet* isn't gonna rhyme with *life*."

"Don't worry, we'll work it out," Ian assured him. "The first step is to get them to agree to our song, so we gotta demo it, right?"

"What's that?" Marc asked, folding his arms.

Ian sighed dramatically. "Lay down the tracks."

Marc looked at him blankly.

"Make a recording of it," Ian explained.

"Oh, yeah, sure. Cool," Marc agreed.

"We'll use my dad's old four-track," Ian decided. "He told me how it works."

"Then what?" William finally spoke up.

"I get my dad to submit it to Westwood Studios for the soundtrack," Ian said confidently as he led the way toward the house and the recording studio in the basement. "And they say yes."

Carrie followed behind as Ian went through his father's office toward the basement door.

"Hey, Carrie!" Ian stopped right near his dad's fax machine. "There's a fax here for you from California! It's from Westwood Studios."

Carrie's heart leapt in her chest. She had been planning to call the studio late that afternoon because of the time difference between Maine and California. Evidently they had beaten her to the punch.

Ian handed the fax to Carrie. "Catch

up with us later, okay?" he asked as he headed off with the other band members. Carrie nodded agreement and then sat down in the office chair to read the fax, which was on Westwood Studios corporate stationery.

Dear Miss Alden:
We received your fax of last night. Mr. London, Jr., passed it on to me because it was transmitted from Graham Perry's fax machine. Don't know how you arranged that. Nice trick.

We love the idea of a teen such as yourself doing a photo shoot of a teen horror movie. I have instructed my publicity staff on the island to offer you every courtesy. The only condition is that your negatives become the property of Westwood Studios. If this is acceptable to you, please countersign this fax below in the space provided and return it to me promptly. I will arrange for press credentials for you.

Sincerely,
Tommy Shih-Goldman
Vice President, Publicity
Westwood Studios

Carrie was in shock. *Too cool!* she thought to herself. *I guess I was right about nothing ventured, nothing gained! Wait till I tell Emma and Sam! They won't believe it! They simply won't believe it!*

THREE

It took forever for Carrie to finally get Ian and Chloe to bed that night, and then Graham and Claudia stayed late at a cocktail party at the home of May Spencer-Rumsey, the publishing magnate. But finally, *finally*, Carrie was obligation-free.

She was out of the house like a flash—she'd planned earlier that evening to meet up with Billy, Sam, and Pres, plus Emma and her boyfriend Kurt Ackerman for a late-night bonfire on the beach. *Not that we need a bonfire, it's still so ridiculously hot*, she thought as she steered Claudia's

Jaguar toward the beach.

When she got there she easily found her friends—they were all sitting together on a blanket under a makeshift flagpole that someone had rigged up. On top of the flagpole was a banner that read "Flirting with Danger." Painted on it was the logo the band had used when out on tour. The banner flapped a bit in the warm night breeze.

"No need for a fire, I see," Carrie said with a smile as she approached her friends.

"Sit down, girlfriend!" Sam cried. "Hey, cute shorts," she added, eyeing Carrie's baggy black-and-white–checked cotton shorts.

"Thanks," Carrie said, flopping down on the blanket. Billy pulled her close and gave her a quick hug.

"Hey, what do you think of the uni?" Sam asked, jumping up and spinning around to show Carrie what she was wearing. "Is it a hoot or what?"

Sam had on giant pink cutoff overalls

with one side unbuckled. Underneath she wore a bra-top covered with teeny little Minnie Mouses blowing kisses.

"You're the only person I know who could pull that off," Carrie said with a laugh. "I'd look like Godzilla in it," she added, staring ruefully at her own full figure.

"Oh, puh-leeze," Sam scoffed. "You are not fat and you have hooters I would kill for."

The guys cracked up and Carrie blushed. "You are hopeless, you know that, don't you?"

"To know me is to love me," Sam agreed.

Emma leaned toward Carrie. "You think she's trying to talk us into it?"

"That's my best guess," Carrie agreed.

"Well, as far as I'm concerned, all three of you are gorgeous," Kurt said, hugging Emma from behind. She settled back happily into his arms.

"Wow, look at that moon," Sam said, staring up at the sky. "Back in Kansas they call it a harvest moon." She looked over at her friends. "And thank God I'm not back in Kansas, I might add."

"I'll drink to that!" Carrie said with a laugh. "What's in the cooler?"

"Coke, juice, wine coolers," Pres said. "What you want?"

"Juice, I guess," Carrie replied.

Pres opened the cooler and tossed Carrie a small bottle of cold apple juice.

"You guys won't believe what happened today," Carrie said to them. "The infamous Lord Whitehead and the Zit People tried to write a song for the *Sunset Beach Slaughter* soundtrack."

"Was it awful?" Emma asked.

"Worse than that, even," Carrie said.

"Well, if Graham wants the song in the movie, Ian will probably have his first film soundtrack credit," Billy said with a shrug.

"Oh, come on," Sam said. "I don't believe that."

"Believe it," Billy assured her. "Power is everything in the music business, and no one has more power than Graham."

"So you think Graham can arrange for them to make me a star?" Sam asked contemplatively.

"Oh, you fixin' to be in the movie now?" Pres drawled in his Tennessee twang.

Sam harrumphed. "Not *fixin'* to be—as you so quaintly put it—*will* be," she corrected. "I bought a killer new bathing suit today at the Cheap Boutique."

"Sam!" Emma exclaimed. "I thought you were on a budget!"

"Emma Cresswell, a girl as rich as you are should never let the word *budget* pass her lips."

Emma shot Sam a look.

"Anyway, I had to buy it," Sam continued defensively. "If I don't get into this movie, it's not going to be because I didn't get noticed by the director!"

"Just how teeny-weeny is this new bathing suit?" Pres wondered.

"Even teenier than what your imagination is conjuring up right now," Sam said, kissing Pres.

"Smoking!" Billy hooted with a laugh.

"Well, I'll be sure to take lots of pictures of you," Carrie told Sam nonchalantly.

"What do you mean?" Emma asked Carrie.

"Just that I'm going to be doing a photo shoot of the movie for Westwood Studios," Carrie said casually.

"Get out of here!" Sam exclaimed.

"It's true!" Carrie insisted jubilantly. She told her friends the whole story of how she managed to snag the photo shoot credential from Westwood Studios.

"That is so great, Car," Billy said, hugging Carrie close. "I'm really proud of you."

"You are?" Carrie asked. *I didn't expect him to say that.*

"Sure am," Billy said. "What you did took guts. And you pulled it off."

"Well—"

"Well nothing," Billy murmured. "Brains and guts are two of the things I love best about you."

"Thanks," Carrie said. "Does this mean

you don't just want me for my body?"

"Well, that, too," Billy admitted with a grin. He gave her a soft, lingering kiss.

Bliss, Carrie thought to herself. *Complete and total bliss.*

"I'm gonna be a star!" Sam yelled, running toward Carrie, waving a newspaper in her hand.

It was the next morning. Carrie was hanging out near the pool of the Sunset Country Club watching Chloe splash around in the shallow wading pool. Sam was followed by Becky and Allie Jacobs, the precocious fourteen-year-old twins whom Sam took care of.

That's the first time I've ever seen Sam voluntarily holding a newspaper, Carrie thought wryly to herself.

"This is it! This is everything!" Sam exulted when she reached Carrie. "I'm gonna be the hugest, most mega-star ever!"

"Correction!" Becky Jacobs yelled, her

hands on her hips. "*I'm* going to be a star. *You* are going to be overlooked."

"Correction again!" Allie Jacobs chimed in. "*I'm* going to be the star. *You* two are going to be getting me Cokes."

"Could I ask what's going on?" Carrie asked mildly, keeping half an eye on Chloe.

"Here!" Sam said, thrusting the newspaper under Carrie's nose. Carrie could see it was the morning edition of the *Portland Press-Herald*'s "Living" section.

Carrie started to scan the page, but Sam yanked the paper away from her. "What it says is that Reginald London intends to do some casting of his movie right here on Sunset Island!" Sam cried gleefully, practically dancing around the pool.

"And I'm gonna be in it!" Allie and Becky squealed at the same time.

The twins turned on each other and glared. "No, you're not!" they shouted at the same time.

"Give it a rest," Sam instructed them. She sat on the edge of Carrie's lounge chair.

"Here, read it!" She thrust the paper back at Carrie.

Carrie took the paper back from Sam. Sure enough, there was an article about the shooting of the film on Sunset Island, and it contained a single line stating that the director was open to casting some bit parts right on the island. Carrie also noticed there was an extensive sidebar article about Molly's parents, the screenwriters.

"They still aren't saying who's starring in it," Carrie noticed, carefully watching Chloe.

"That's because they don't know I'm in it yet," Sam decided.

"I don't think that's very realistic," Carrie said, pulling her sunblock out of her bag.

"Realism never turned anyone into a movie star," Sam pointed out. "I understand Lana Turner got discovered sitting at a drugstore counter in Hollywood."

"Who's she?" Allie asked, puzzled.

"A famous actress from the forties," Carrie told her.

44

"Never heard of her," Becky reported dismissively. "My favorite is Samantha Mathis."

"Samantha Bridges will make them forget all about Samantha Mathis," Sam pontificated. "I can just see it now—makeup crews swarming around, flunkies at my beck and call, bringing me anything I want, a cellular phone—"

"I don't care who the male lead is," Allie Jacobs rhapsodized, "as long as it's Luke Perry." She and Becky made kissing noises until Sam shushed them.

"Anyway," Sam said, "this article just confirms it for me."

"Confirms what?" Carrie queried, spreading the sunblock on her legs.

"Confirms that the next several days are going to be a turning point in my life," Sam announced. "I mean, Westwood Studios is a big studio."

"Listen, Sam," Becky said slowly, as if she were speaking to a foreigner, "this is a teen movie."

"Yeah, a teen movie," Allie agreed. "And we're the teens!"

"I'm nineteen," Sam reminded the twins.

"Yeah, you're practically an adult!" Becky added. "Like, over the hill!"

Sam merely smiled a beautific smile in the face of this abuse from the twins.

"Girls," she finally said sweetly, "we have to go. You both need to get home for lunch because you're starting to get cranky."

Allie and Becky hissed at Sam, who winked at Carrie and headed off.

"See you tonight?" Sam yelled back to Carrie.

"Where?" Carrie asked.

"Play Café, usual table, usual hour."

"I'll be there," Carrie assured her.

"You'll recognize me," Sam yelped. "I'll be the one with the paparazzi swarming around."

Carrie grinned and waved. *That gives me an idea,* she thought to herself as she watched Chloe playing some water game with a little boy. *They start shoot-*

46

ing this movie tomorrow. That means all the setup and advance people should be arriving this afternoon. And if they arrive, the stars should arrive, too. I'd better be ready for anything.

Carrie resolved that no matter where she went, starting that very day, her cameras were going to be secure around her neck.

"Her name is Cindi Etheridge," Claudia said to Carrie as she stood in the kitchen slicing vegetables for a salad. "And I want you to pick her up on the six o'clock ferry."

It was late that afternoon, and Claudia had just finished telling Carrie about how she had gotten a surprise phone call around noontime from an old friend of hers from when was growing up in Michigan.

"You know, one of those people you sort of get out of touch with but is still your friend," Claudia said to Carrie, as if Carrie was a buddy instead of an employee. "When we were teenagers we were as

47

close as you and Sam and Emma are right now."

"That's nice," Carrie said politely. Inside, though, she knew better. *I would never, ever lose touch with Sam and Emma,* Carrie thought to herself. *They mean everything to me. And they always will.*

"It's funny," Claudia mused, reaching for a tomato. "There was a time when I believed we'd be best friends forever, and then we just drifted apart."

Well, if you just "drifted apart," you couldn't have really been best friends, Carrie thought.

"I guess you think that could never happen to you," Claudia said. She smiled at Carrie. "Enjoy your best friends before your life gets too complicated for them."

Carrie suddenly remembered that Claudia and Cindi were only in their twenties—Ian was from Graham's first marriage. *How could things have changed that much for them?* "So how will I recognize her at the ferry?" Carrie asked.

Claudia laughed. "You'll recognize her. Cindi always had her own style. In her case, it was black clothes. She told me that didn't change."

"How long's it been since you saw her?" Carrie asked, washing some lettuce for the salad.

"A really long time . . . five years, I think," Claudia said with a sigh. "She just called me . . . out of the blue, really. She said something on the phone about a divorce, and having to get away from it all, so she took the car and drove to Maine, and here she is."

Carrie raised her eyebrows. "Sounds complicated."

"Yeah," Claudia agreed. She turned to look at Carrie. "I guess you're wondering why I'm not going to meet her myself, since she's my friend and everything."

"It's none of my business," Carrie said, even though she'd been wondering that exact thing.

"I guess I'm a little nervous about this," Claudia admitted. "That's why I asked you to get her. I'm just hoping it won't be too weird, seeing her again."

Carrie looked at her watch. Five-forty P.M. If she was going to meet the six o'clock ferry, she'd have to hurry.

"I gotta go," Carrie said.

"Remember," Claudia said, "Cindi Etheridge. Black clothes. About five feet five. Average weight and height. Average everything."

Sort of like me, Carrie thought. But she didn't say anything. Instead, she grabbed the car keys and her cameras—she remembered her vow to herself of earlier that day—and was gone.

By the time Carrie drove to the Sunset Island ferryport, the six o'clock ferry from Portland was just pulling in. Carrie could see it was loaded to the gills—and not just with people but with what looked like motor homes, vans, and trucks full of equipment.

Of course! Carrie thought. *It's all the equipment for the movie.* She quickly unslung one of her cameras from around her neck and started shooting. As the ferry docked and was being tied into port, Carrie took an entire roll of film using her telephoto lens.

Finally passengers started pouring off the ferry. And what passengers! *Look at those outfits! Sam would be so jealous!* Carrie watched as really good-looking young women and men dressed in the height of Los Angeles fashion headed onto the island. The women were in gauze and mesh bra-tops worn with the tightest white jeans Carrie had ever seen, with high heels to match. The guys sported similar jeans, but with plain white T-shirts.

Heels with jeans? Carrie thought, watching the girls mince their way out of the boat. *That is so uncool on Sunset Island!*

Then three of the longest stretch limos Carrie had ever seen pulled off the ferry. Carrie tried to peer inside them to see whose they were, but she couldn't even catch a glimpse of the passengers.

Finally, after practically all the passengers had disembarked, an attractive woman in her mid to late-twenties, with very short black hair, an all-black sundress, and a black baseball cap with a big X on it, got off the boat, looking around uncertainly. She was carrying a small duffel bag.

That's her, Carrie thought. *That's got to be her.*

Carrie approached the woman.

"Cindi Etheridge?" Carrie asked.

The woman looked a little startled.

"Yes?" she replied.

"Hi, I'm Carrie Alden," Carrie said. "I work for Claudia Templeton. She asked me to pick you up." Carrie stuck out her hand, and Cindi shook it automatically.

"Oh," Cindi said, looking a little disappointed. "I thought Claudia said—" Then Cindi's face brightened. "No matter. I got to the ferry a little late. They wouldn't let me take my car on. Too crowded."

"It can happen," Carrie said. "Follow me." She headed for the Templetons' Mercedes, and Cindi silently trotted along next to her.

Well, this is weird, Carrie thought. *I can't think of a single thing to say.*

Cindi didn't seem to be feeling talkative, either. So they made the short drive to the Templetons' in total silence. Finally Carrie pulled into the driveway.

"Well, here we are!" she said brightly.

"This place is incredible," Cindi breathed, staring at the huge mansion.

"Yeah, I guess it is, at that," Carrie agreed. They got out of the car. "So, are you excited about seeing Claudia?" she asked, just to try to make some conversation.

"The truth?" Cindi asked, looking sharply at Carrie.

"Sure," Carrie said with a shrug.

Cindi's face clouded over and she inhaled sharply. "I'm scared to death."

FOUR

"Claudia?" Cindi said as she stuck her head through the front door of the Templetons' house.

"Cinder!" Claudia yelped as she came flying out of the kitchen. Carrie watched as Cindi and Claudia embraced like long-lost sisters.

"No one's called me that since . . . well, since I saw you last," Cindi realized with a nervous laugh. She looked around her in awe. "What a place!"

"Oh, it's just home!" Claudia said brightly.

"Just home, nothing," Cindi scoffed. She

pointed to a large painting on the wall of the huge entryway. "That's an original Helnwein!"

"Well, it's just a painting!" Claudia said easily.

"A painting worth a small fortune," Cindi said with a laugh.

Claudia shrugged and turned away from her friend.

Why, she's really uncomfortable about this, Carrie realized. *She doesn't like her old friend pointing out how rich she is now!*

"Why don't you let Carrie show you to your room," Claudia suggested. "You can take a shower if you want, and then come down for dinner."

"Cool," Cindi agreed, still looking at the painting.

Claudia motioned to Carrie to lead the way upstairs for Cindi.

"Follow me," Carrie said, reaching for Cindi's suitcase.

"Oh, please, I'll take it," Cindi insisted,

and she did. Carrie led her up to one of the huge guest bedrooms on the second floor, showed her where her private bath was, and then excused herself. By the time Carrie was headed back downstairs to the kitchen, she could already hear the sound of running water in the shower.

Back in the kitchen Claudia was setting the table for dinner. Carrie came in and started helping her.

"I suppose you're curious about Cindi and me," Claudia said to her.

"A little," Carrie admitted honestly, getting the glasses from the cupboard.

"She's one of the smartest people I've ever met. And all those smarts never did her any good," Claudia said with a sigh.

Carrie nodded. *Well, I sure feel funny having Claudia confide in me like we're buddies,* she realized. *I guess she just needs someone to talk to. Gee, you never know what's in the job description,* Carrie thought wryly.

"Cindi's a writer, you know," Claudia explained.

"I didn't know," Carrie responded.

"Uh-huh."

"What does she write?"

Claudia set out some wineglasses on the table. "Nonfiction, mostly for magazines. She's a specialist on art and the art market."

That explains why she immediately knew that painting, Carrie thought.

"Who does she write for?" Carrie asked while looking for the good cloth napkins for the table.

"Oh, some art magazines. *Art and Auction* I think is one of them," Claudia answered. "I can't say it's something I know that much about."

"She was one of your best friends?" Carrie asked, still a little in disbelief that Claudia, a grown woman, would allow herself to grow apart from someone she said was once her best friend.

"Yup," Claudia said.

"So what happened?" Carrie asked, even before she could stop herself from prying.

"Well," Claudia answered, not at all taken aback by Carrie's question, "it was just one of those things. I went to New York to work for Polimar, Cindi went to college at Southern Cal, I got married, then she got married . . . you know."

No, I don't know, Carrie thought.

"So what's the story on her now?" Carrie finally asked.

"I really don't know," Claudia confessed. "She called me . . . like, out of the blue."

"But you're glad to see her, aren't you?" Carrie asked.

"Sure," Claudia replied not too convincingly.

"So, did she call you just to rekindle your friendship?" Carrie asked.

"I guess I'll find that out soon," Claudia said. "Won't I?"

"The thing is," Carrie said to Emma and Sam, "we never did get the story on Cindi.

All through dinner they talked about stupid stuff like the weather and what movies they'd seen!"

It was four hours later, and Carrie was back at her usual place in the Play Café with Sam and Emma. The café was packed, and everyone was buzzing with rumors and news about *Sunset Beach Slaughter*. Carrie had just finished recounting to her friends the arrival of Cindi Etheridge at the Templeton house.

"Well," sniffed Sam, "that hardly makes them best friends. I mean, that's the kind of stuff I talk about with my *sister*."

"It surprised me, too," Carrie admitted.

"It certainly doesn't say much for Claudia," Sam added, reaching into a basket of french fries and taking out a handful.

"That's easy for you to say," Emma suggested. "You don't even know this Cindi person."

"I know that I would never ever treat you or Carrie like that," Sam said emphatically, still chewing on the french fries. "Even if Carrie here has no late-night fashion sense. Where'd you get that outfit?"

Carrie looked down at what she was wearing. A super-baggy pair of orange cotton shorts and a long-sleeve white sweatshirt that read "COPE: The Future of Sunset Island."

"This is okay," Carrie said with a shrug.

"Yes," Sam said haughtily. "Okay if you want to blend into the crowd. But not okay if you want to get noticed by a major Hollywood studio." With that, Sam stood up and removed the Flirting with Danger satin tour jacket she was wearing.

"Ta-da!" she cried and circled around for her friends. She had on a see-through leopard-print camisole with a black bra underneath it, plus black denim short-shorts with pieces cut out where leopard material had been inserted. The shorts were held up with a narrow black velvet belt that looped closed and then hung down, a leopard print point on the very end. Instead of Sam's usual red cowboy boots, she wore ankle-high black cowboy boot-shoes.

"Wow," Carrie said.

"Only you could get away with wearing that in public," Emma opined.

"Without getting arrested," Carrie added.

"Hey, this uni is tame by Hollywood standards," Sam said, sitting back down. "If Reginald London the Third comes into the Play Café tonight, I am prepared."

"Well, I'm sure he'd notice you," Emma said loyally.

"Hey, we all work with our long suit," Sam said with a shrug, reaching for some more french fries. "I mean, look at you, Carrie, you're prepared." Sam pointed to Carrie's camera bag on the floor. The strap from the bag was wrapped around Carrie's ankle, to prevent anyone from grabbing it and running off.

"You never know when you're going to find a great picture," Carrie said. "Hey, maybe I'll get a picture of you and Reginald London together!"

"How about me and Emma and Reginald London together?" Sam cracked. "Reggie and me, hand in hand, and Emma clearing the fans out of the way."

"I live to serve, O Fashionable One," Emma said with a mock bow.

Sam laughed. "Wow, can you imagine—"

She was interrupted by a tremendous commotion in front of the café. Carrie could just see the side of a white stretch limousine through the open door.

Maybe Sam's wish is about to come true!

As the girls' attention was riveted to the front of the café, the crowd began to buzz even louder. Then it parted, as if it had been cut by a knife. Two enormous men, each well over six feet, dressed in designer warm-up suits, came into the café, looked around, and then gave some sort of signal back to the limo. Then the limo door opened again. Out stepped a young man of medium height, slender and well built, his hair swept back from his forhead, long side-burns emphasizing his chiseled features.

"Oh-mi-God-oh-mi-God," Sam chanted. "I am going to die this very minute." She grabbed Carrie's arm so hard that Carrie winced. "That's Jake Creston!" she screeched.

"That's the name of the character he plays on *Hollywood High*," Emma pointed out, her eyes also glued to the front door of the club, "not his real name."

Hollywood High was the top-rated network TV show about teens in the country.

"I know that," Sam whispered. "His real name is Duke Underwood," she added dreamily.

Carrie watched Duke pull off his sun-glasses and look around the Play Café. "Well, you guys, I think we just found out who the secret star of *Slaughter on Sunset Beach* is."

A half hour later the Play Café was back to normal—sort of. Duke Underwood—who

Carrie had to admit looked even better in person than he did on TV—was ensconced at the bar with his bodyguards nearby. He was talking with a gorgeous young woman dressed even more outrageously than Sam—*obviously an actress*, Carrie thought—who came in a few minutes after he did.

"I didn't know he had a girlfriend," Emma said to her friends.

"I thought you didn't watch TV," Carrie quipped.

"I don't," Emma answered, sneaking a glance over at Duke. "But I read *Time* magazine, and the article about him last week said he was unattached."

Sam grinned. "Good for me."

"Don't forget about what happened with Johnny Angel," Carrie cautioned her.

"You're boring me." Sam winked. "Anyway, there's a big difference. Johnny Angel is a musician; Duke is a movie star."

"What's the difference?" Carrie queried,

glancing over at Duke Underwood, who had his back to them.

"I have no idea," Sam admitted. "Why don't you take his picture?"

Carrie shook her head. "Not cool. Not in here."

"Oh, go on," Emma encouraged her. "He's used to it. He probably expects it."

"Well—"

"And make sure you take his picture with us!" Sam added. Sam then reached down for Carrie's camera bag.

Should I? Oh, what the heck. You only live once. I'll tell him I'm doing a photo essay on the movie shoot. I wish I had my credentials, though.

Carrie got up slowly, put her cameras around her neck, and walked over toward Duke Underwood. The girls saw him turn around to face Carrie. They watched Carrie and him have a brief conversation, and then stared in astonishment as Duke followed Carrie back to their table. Duke's bodyguards trotted along behind him.

"Hi, I'm Duke Underwood," Duke said, stretching out his hand. "And your friend—what's your name again?"

"Carrie Alden," Carrie said in as professional a tone of voice as she could muster. *My knees are knocking together. I can't believe this is happening!*

"Right, Carrie—she's the first polite photographer I've met since 1989."

"Samantha Bridges," Sam said, standing up. She was as tall as Duke Underwood. She smiled her most inviting smile.

"Nice to meetcha," Duke said easily.

"Emma Cresswell," Emma said as she stood up, too.

"A pleasure, Emma," Duke mumbled, sticking out his hand distractedly. "Okay, Carrie, let's shoot this, and then I'm outta here."

Carrie fumbled with her flash equipment, snapped off a few pictures of Duke Underwood with Sam and Emma, and then told Duke she'd gotten what she needed.

"Thanks, Carrie," Duke said with genuine warmth in his voice. "I'll see you on location tomorrow." With that, Duke and his entourage turned and left the Play Café.

"He touched me!" Sam yelled. "He knows who I am! Great romances have begun this way!"

"Somebody hose her down!" a girl from the next table yelled.

"Ha! You're just jealous!" Sam called back to the girl, but she sat down and stopped yelling.

"I think I got some good pictures," Carrie ventured. "God, I was scared to death."

"Good job, Carrie," Emma supported her friend. "That took a lot of guts."

"I can't wait until tomorrow," Sam declared solemnly to her friends. "This could be one of the most important nights of my life."

"Sam, don't you ever think of anyone except yourself?" Emma said, a little annoyance in her voice.

"Yes," Sam answered seriously, her tone completely contrite. "I think about Duke Underwood. And tomorrow he's going to be thinking about Samantha Bridges."

FIVE

Carrie reached around her neck one more time to feel for her press credentials, then looked out again over the main beach at Sunset Island. It was the next day, around noontime, and she was watching an almost-unbelievable scene.

The beach was packed with teenagers— it seemed as if every kid who lived within a hundred miles of Sunset Island was there. And, just like an article that had appeared in the *Portland Press-Herald* that morning had instructed, they were all wearing bathing suits. The guys had on mostly multicolored baggy bathing suits, and the girls seemed to be competing in a skimpiest-bikini-in-the-world contest.

Good thing I'm shooting pictures of this, Carrie thought to herself. *I'd never have the nerve to wear one of those teeny bikinis!*

Not only was the beach packed with kids, but there was tons of movie equipment there—even a crane with a camera mounted on it so Reginald London III could get the overhead shots he wanted.

There was a rope separating the shooting crew from the big crowd, and Carrie was on the crew's side of the rope. Just then she saw Emma and Sam approach the rope and look around intently.

They're trying to find me back here, Carrie thought. *Good luck in this madhouse. I'll go to them.*

Carrie threaded her way through the film crew and equipment until her friends caught sight of her.

"Hey, official photog!" Sam cried when Carrie approached. "What do you think of the suit?" Sam spun around to show off her new bikini—it was hot pink with white stars on it. It was the teeniest bikini Carrie had every seen.

"Eye-catching," Carrie reported.

"That's the whole idea!" Sam chortled. "I've got to stand out in the crowd, and stand out I will!"

"Hey, Emma," Carrie said, eyeing her friend, who looked fabulous in an all-white halter-top suit with high-cut legs. "You look great, but I bet you're the only girl here not wearing a bikini!" *Not that anything would look bad on Emma,* Carrie thought to herself. *She has one of those perfectly slender bodies I'd kill for. Leave it to Emma to dress tastefully for a slasher movie!*

"Thanks," Emma said gratefully. "Sam had to talk me into coming."

"Yeah, like it was tough," Sam joked.

"You know what drives me nuts about this?" Emma asked, looking around at the hoards of teen hopefuls. "The guys are dressed in perfectly normal bathing suits, but the girls are wearing next to nothing!"

"Yeah, it's your basic sexist cattle call," Sam agreed, as if she'd been to dozens before. "If women ran Hollywood, I bet you'd see the guys here wearing those teeny little French racing bikinis!"

Emma sighed. "Whatever happened to understated elegance?"

Carrie laughed and threw her arm around Emma's shoulder's sympathetically. "Honestly, Em, you missed your era."

"Yeah, girlfriend," Sam agreed. Remember, the days of Princess Grace are over!"

Carrie looked around. "So where are Darcy and Molly and the guys?" She knew Billy had zero interest in being in a big teen party scene on the beach, but she wasn't sure what Kurt and Pres were doing.

"Molly came down with the flu and Darcy's taking care of her, and Kurt's at the club, working," Emma reported.

"Pres is working on his bike," Sam said, "so I guess it's just me and Duke Underwood. What a pity. Where is he, anyway?"

"In his trailer," Carrie said, motioning over her shoulder to a row of RVs parked in a line on the beach.

"Who else has one?" Emma asked.

"That pro wrestler, Rocky Mountain, who's playing the cook," Carrie said. "You should see, the guy is about ten feet tall and weighs about a million pounds."

"Introduce him to Diana," Sam joked. "As long as he zips his pants at the crotch, she'll go for him."

"Who else?" Emma questioned.

"That girl we saw in Play Café last night," Carrie added. "Her name is Lily Vallez."

"Lily Vallez?" Sam repeated. "You mean like Lily of the Valley with a French pronunciation?"

"You got it," Carrie confirmed.

"I bet she was born Lorraine Valeski or something," Sam snorted.

Carrie shrugged. "She's from Alabama.

This is her second feature and her first big lead. She plays the girl who actually kills the slasher at the end of the movie."

"I wish it were me." Sam sighed. "What has she got that I haven't got?"

"The part?" Emma suggested sweetly.

"Well, yeah," Sam admitted. "But I mean other than that."

"She was a model, doing TV commercials in New York, when someone discovered her," Carrie told them.

"How do you happen to have all this info?" Emma asked curiously.

"Oh, it came with my press stuff," Carrie explained.

"*Attention! Attention!*" A voice rang out over a loudspeaker system that had been set up on the beach.

The girls all stopped talking to listen. The voice continued to speak after a brief pause.

"*Good Morning! I'm Reginald London the Third, the director of* Sunset Beach Slaughter . . .*"

"And here I thought it was *Gone With the Wind*," Sam cracked.

"Shush," Emma quieted her.

"*—so thanks for wanting to take part in my film.*"

" 'My film'?" Sam joked again. "I thought it was a Westwood Studios movie."

"That's how directors talk," Emma said quickly, then moved to quiet Sam again.

"*I expect to redefine this genre of motion picture with* Sunset Beach Slaughter. *Never forget that this is art we are making here. Now, my intent in this take is to get the sense of an enormous party on the beach—lots of teen decadence, drinking, et cetera, et cetera. Please use your imaginations. Do not look at the cameras as they go by. I will be using this footage in various places in my movie. You are the decadent youth of America. Show me your stuff. We will begin filming in ten minutes.*"

"Hey!" some girl yelled out from the crowd. "Mr. London! I think this is totally bogus! How come all the guys have on these baggy suits while all the girls are wearing next to nothing?"

"Who yelled that question? Who?"

Carrie and her friends watched as some college-age girl with spiky dark hair pushed her way to the restraining rope and raised her hand.

"Young lady, where do you go to college?"

"Hofstra!" she shouted.

"Take a film class! This is art happening here. And take a hike off my set. Anyone else have anything to say? No one? Good. My set is not a democracy."

No one else said a word, and the spiky-haired girl slunk off the beach, a scowl on her face.

Emma could barely contain herself from laughing. "What does he think he's doing, making an Academy Award-winner?"

"As a matter of fact, yes! And another word from you and you're off my set, too."

Carrie and her friends swung around. Reginald London III was rolling on top of a flatbed truck not twenty feet from where they were standing. Carrie quickly swung back so that he couldn't see her press credentials, but by then the flatbed truck had passed.

"What a jerk," Sam muttered.

"I'm sorry I even came," Emma agreed. "Want to go?"

"Well, he's not that much of a jerk," Sam amended.

"I'd better get to work," Carrie told her friends. "Have fun!"

After getting the permission of the camera person and his assistant, Carrie climbed to the top of a platform that had been erected for one of the cameras. She watched, amazed, as some of the production assistants got ready for the scene. And then she started clicking away with her camera.

She took pictures of assistants dumping huge garbage bags full of empty beer cans on the beach, to make it look as if a wild party was underway. She took pictures as the assistants handed out emptied beer cans that had been filled with root beer so that the kids could shake the cans up and squirt root beer on one another.

"You kids know what to do with these?" an assistant asked as he handed out fake marijuana cigarettes.

"Gee, no," one blond kid said sarcastically.

"Hey, mind if we substitute the real thing?" his friend called out loudly.

A bunch of kids around them laughed. Carrie snapped away with her camera.

"Yeah, I mind a lot," the assistant said. "No druggies allowed on the set. If I smell the real stuff, you're in big trouble." He reached into a bag and took out some packs of cigarettes. "Okay, smokers, take these Camels and light up when you get the word."

"Bogus, man," a guy in the crowd said. "No one smokes cigarettes anymore."

"Look, this is show biz, so smoke," the assistant said tersely.

Carrie snapped away. Someone turned

on a sound system, and raucous rap music blasted across the beach.

"Crowd!" came the loud voice through the sound system. *"Begin to boogie. We need some setup boogie shots!"*

Everyone on the beach began to dance, yell, and run around, as if a huge party were in progress.

This has as much to do with real life as The Wizard of Oz, Carrie thought grimly, but she snapped away diligently.

After about ten minutes Reginald London's voice rang out again over the sound system.

"Cut! Cut! Cut! That'll do it. Okay, kids, that's it for the guys. Off the beach. Off! Girls, you stay here."

Carrie clicked away as about two hundred young men grudgingly left the beach. Most of them stayed up along the boardwalk to see what happened next.

"This next scene is a swimming scene. I want all the girls to gather around my assistant, Connie. She's the one standing

holding the ten-foot-high pole. Now!"

The hundreds of girls ran and pushed their way near Connie, jockeying for position.

"Good. Now, let us get in position."

A couple of flatbed trucks, one containing Reginald London III, worked their way toward the waterline. One of them came dangerously close to bogging down in the sand, but it finally made it.

"Groovy. Now, on my count of five, I want the whole group of you to run toward the water, dive in, and start splashing around. Be sure you jump up and down a lot. Can you do that? Good. Now, one, two, three—"

Carrie saw Sam push her way closest to the water so she'd be the first girl filmed.

"Five!"

The whole group of teens—maybe about three hundred girls—ran at a breakneck pace toward the water. Carrie clicked shot after shot as they dived into the chilly Maine ocean and started splashing each other. Carrie could see that Sam had led the way.

"Cut! Cut! Cut! *No good. I want a differ-ent girl in the front. Not that big redhead. Somebody move the redhead!*"

As Carrie watched, an underling ran over to Sam and took her by the arm, moving her to the center of the crowd of girls.

"*Much better. Okay, I need someone who speaks to me in the front. Let me look you all over down there....*"

A hush came over the crowd of girls as each one hoped that the director was about to select her. Carrie watched Sam turn away completely and fold her arms. *I hope she's more angry than humiliated,* Carrie thought.

"*I'm looking for a girl who conveys every-thing with just her eyes ... and there she is! Yes, you! The one with the body! What's your name?*"

Carrie looked over at the girl at whom Reginald was pointing, and she groaned.

"Diana De Witt," Diana called up to the director sexily. "But you can call me Diana."

Oh, God—Diana. Sam'll never live this down, Carrie thought— *getting passed over for Diana!*

"Well, Diana," boomed Reginald London, "this is your lucky day! You lead it! Okay, let's all reassemble by Connie. Good. Now, on my count of five, run to the water. I don't care if you're already wet. One, two, three, four, five!"

Carrie watched again as Diana DeWitt led the whole group of girls down into the ocean. Sam, this time, was somewhere near the middle of the pack. And she didn't seem too enthusiastic about getting back in the ocean.

"Okay! Cut! It's a wrap. Thanks, girls. You were incredible!"

Well, I think I got some great stuff, Carrie thought to herself as she walked over to have a seat under the boardwalk. She sat down to change film. *But if this is movie-making, I don't want any part of it.* She looked at her watch. It was one-thirty. She had an hour and a half before she had to get back to the Templetons' to babysit for Chloe.

Carrie was having some trouble with her film, so she didn't even notice the people streaming by her to leave the film shoot. In fact, she was so absorbed she didn't even notice the large wharf rat that had come out from under the boardwalk and was nibbling on a torn candy wrapper at her feet.

She didn't notice the rat until it brushed up against her leg. She glanced down. And she screamed. Loud. She jumped up and ran out from under the boardwalk, smack into Reginald London III. And knocked him right down.

"Oh, I'm so sorry," Carrie apologized. "I mean, really, really sorry."

Reginald London got up, brushed the sand off himself, and looked at Carrie closely.

"I . . . I apologize," Carrie repeated, brushing at the director's shirt. "I don't know how I could have been so stupid. I mean, it was only a rat!"

Only a rat—how dumb does that sound? He's probably going to take away my credentials and make me quit or something. And I probably deserve it. Carrie was so distraught that she couldn't look Reginald in the eye.

When she finally looked up, Reginald London was smiling at her.

Uh, oh, here it comes. He's going to tell me to get off the project, and he's going to do it with a smile on his face.

"You're the photographer, right?" he asked.

"Yes," Carrie said, wishing she were a million miles away from Sunset Island.

"That's quite a scream you have," he noted.

"Well, I try not to do it often," Carrie replied with a weak smile.

"Hmmm," Reginald said, narrowing his eyes at Carrie. "Turn around."

"Pardon me?" Carrie asked.

"Just turn around, please," Reginald repeated.

Carrie sighed and dutifully turned around. *I guess this is so he can tell me to walk back in the direction I came from and keep walking until I'm off his set,* Carrie figured.

"Marvelous," Reginald cooed. "Now turn back to me."

Carrie turned. "Look, if you want to fire me just do it. There's no point in—"

"Right scream, right look, right build, could be perfect-amundo," Reginald murmured.

"Excuse me?" Carrie asked.

"What's your name?" Reginald asked.

"Carrie Alden," Carrie replied, completely confused.

"Well, Carrie Alden, this might just be your lucky day!" the director said with a grin.

"I'm really not following you," Carrie admitted.

"I mean, Carrie Alden," Reginald said portentously, "how would you like to be in a movie?"

SIX

"What are you talking about?" Carrie asked, genuinely baffled.

"That scream, that look, that disingenuity—like Jean Seberg in *Breathless*. Yes, it's perfect!" Reginald said, his voice rising with enthusiasm.

"What is *Breathless*?" Carrie asked. "And who is Jean Seberg?"

"Oh, Carrie Alden," Reginald continued, "some may say that all my movie will be is another exploitation film—some nonothings will even call it a *sex*-ploitation film—but you and I know different, don't we?"

I'd better go along with him because he has the power to take away my press credentials if he gets temperamental, and I've seen him get temperamental! "Sure," she agreed gamely. Then she moved a bit to her left, to avoid three burly men carrying some heavy equipment off the beach.

"Oh, you are so coy!" Reginald said with a wicked laugh. "I love it!"

Carrie smiled and tried not to let on what she was thinking. *This guy is a total lunatic.*

"Remember *Phantom of the Opera*, where the Phantom lurked in the Paris Opera House, misguided and misunderstood?" Reginald continued eagerly. "Why, that's the role Rocky Mountain is playing. Only he does his killing in broad daylight!"

This guy has got to be kidding, Carrie thought. Sunset Beach Slaughter *doesn't have a great deal to do with* The Phantom of the Opera. *It's more like* The Texas Chainsaw Massacre.

"I see," Carrie said noncommittally.

"Of course you do!" Reginald London chortled. "And that's why it's important that she be absolutely perfect!"

"She?" Carrie asked. "I thought Rocky Mountain was playing the slasher."

"Not the killer," Reginald London said, his tone getting a little supercilious. "The killee. The girl whom the slasher offs. The first death of the film."

"Oh," Carrie said.

"You," Reginald pointed.

"Who?"

"You," he repeated, pointing right at Carrie. "Carrie Alden, victim number one."

"Me?"

"Of course!" Reginald cried. "You're perfect."

"I am?" Carrie asked.

"And modest, too! That subtext of modesty under the skin of the floozy. It will just make the crime more human," Reginald continued with a flourish, as if he were teaching a course on film theory at UCLA.

"You want me in the movie?" Carrie said,

starting to comprehend what Reginald was saying. "To be the first victim that Rocky Mountain murders?"

"Close your eyes," Reginald ordered.

"What?" Carrie asked.

"Close your eyes!"

Carrie closed her eyes.

"Imagine, if you will, you are now Lucinda Kittyn—everyone calls you Luce. Your father owns the Slay Café, and now you work there as a waitress. For years—since you were a small child—Grisly Arnold, disfigured cook, has had a terrible crush on you. You've always been kind to him—you see the man inside the monster—and yet at the same time he repulses you."

Carrie snuck her eyes open and risked a peek at Reginald. Fortunately he was lost in painting his cinematic picture. She quickly snapped her eyes shut again.

"Now you've grown up, Miss Luce Kittyn," the director continued. "You are a curvy, luscious woman, and Grisly can't be restrained. He wants you, wants you desperately. But you reject him. He can't take it anymore. So one night he comes for you and—"

"Kills me," Carrie finished, opening her eyes.

"Something like that. But more arty," Reginald assured Carrie.

"Arty," Carrie repeated.

Reginald nodded. "You must say yes," he implored Carrie. "You *are* Luce Kittyn!"

"Look, I really appreciate your interest," Carrie began carefully. "But I'm not an actress—"

"That's good, that's what I want!" Reginald insisted. "My movie is screaming for realism!"

"But . . . there are hundreds of girls prettier than me just dying to be in your picture," Carrie tried again. "In fact, I have a good friend who would be perfect—"

"I don't want perfect," the director insisted. "You look real—that is my whole point! I'm sick unto death of this Hollywood glitz. I must have you!"

I can't believe this is happening, Carrie thought. *This wacko is not going to be interested in taking no for an answer. He has his heart set on me being Luce Kittyn. If I don't do it, he's apt to have a temper tantrum and toss me off the set. If I do it, I'll probably get inside access to any photographs I want . . .*

"How long is this going to take?" Carrie asked.

"About an hour," Reginald said. "Day after tomorrow. Very early."

"I'll call you," Carrie said.

"We'll pay you five thousand bucks," Reginald added, nonchalantly.

"I'm there," Carrie said quickly.

"Knew you'd see it my way," Reginald said. "Call my assistant on the mobile tomorrow. She'll give you details." He took out a card in his pocket and gave it to Carrie. Carrie looked at the card. On it were about five phone numbers, and one of them had the word *Mobile* next to it.

"Okay," Carrie agreed.

"Groovy," Reginald said with a grin. "And I promise, no total nudity!"

"What?" Carrie yelped. "Who said anything about—"

But Reginald couldn't hear her since he was hurrying off with two or three assistants.

"Who said anything about any kind of nudity?" she asked out loud.

Unfortunately, there was no one there to answer her.

"Carrie—you're kidding," Emma said finally.

"Nope," Carrie responded, cradling the telephone against her shoulder as she rolled back on her bed and stuck her legs up against the wall. "Do you think I could make that story up?" She laughed at the absurdity of it all.

It was later that afternoon, and while Chloe took a nap, Carrie was taking a few minutes to call Emma to talk over Reginald London III's offer to put her in *Sunset Beach*

Slaughter, in an actual speaking role! She couldn't stay on long, though, because it was already almost five, and Claudia had left her a note asking her to put some hors d'oeuvres in the oven for her and Cindi before they came back from the beach.

"This is hilarious!" Emma cried. "Have you told Sam yet?"

"Are you kidding?" Carrie asked. "I thought I would leave that for you to do, after how Reginald totally humiliated her on the beach today."

"Aw, come on," Emma cajoled, "she'll be happy for you."

"I don't know," Carrie said. "She'd do anything to get a speaking role in this movie. Anything."

"I hope not," Emma reflected. "Well, maybe she'll be so mad at that director she won't be jealous."

"Right," Carrie responded. "And maybe the Zit People will actually place one of their songs on the soundtrack album."

"Billy seems to think that could actually

happen," Emma reminded Carrie.

"Scary thought," Carrie mused.

"So you're actually going to do this?" Emma asked.

"Emma, it pays five thousand dollars!"

"Wow," Emma breathed.

"Do you know how much that will help with my expenses in the fall?"

"Lots," Emma agreed.

"And, I mean, how sleazy could it be?" Carrie asked. "He promised me no total nudity."

"That doesn't count out partial nudity," Emma warned.

"Well, it does for me," Carrie said. "Can you imagine someone as self-conscious about her body as me appearing partially nude on a twenty-foot movie screen? It would be like my worst nightmare come true!"

"So you'll just tell him no if it comes up," Emma said.

"Right," Carrie agreed. "I'm not signing anything that says I have to wear anything less than what I wear on the beach."

"Good for you," Emma approved. "And don't worry about Sam. I know she's going to be happy for you."

Carrie looked at her watch. "I gotta run now—Claudia's coming home soon with her old friend."

"Okay," Emma said, "I'll see you later. Will you be free tonight? Darcy and Molly called to say there's going to be a big party at the Masons' place. Around nine."

"Who knows?" Carrie answered. "Graham and Claudia have been going out a lot lately, which means I've been home a lot. Anyway, I'll call you. Bye!"

Emma said good-bye, and Carrie hung up the phone.

I'm actually going to be in a movie. A movie with Duke Underwood. As Sam would say: Whoa, baby!

Then she had an awful thought. What if she couldn't get the time off from work to do the movie?

But Claudia and Graham will have to

understand how much it means to me to make that kind of money for college, she told herself. *And the shoot won't take that much time. I'm sure they won't stand in my way. I hope.*

Carrie looked in the mirror and assessed herself. *Not Emma, and not Sam, but not bad,* she thought. She was wearing a flower-print sundress and a straw hat with a violet in the front that matched the dress. She slung a couple of cameras around her neck and pronounced herself ready for the party at the Masons. She grabbed the keys to the spare Mercedes and was off.

A few hours earlier Claudia had called to tell her that not only were she and Cindi not having hors d'oeuvres or dinner at home, but that they were just stopping by to change and pick up Chloe, then meet Graham and Ian at the Sunset Country Club to eat. That freed Carrie up to go to the party.

The bad news is that I didn't get to talk to Graham and Claudia about whether I can get the time to do the movie shoot. Oh, well, I'll catch them in the morning.

When Carrie got to the Masons' house on the hill, the party was in full swing. Because it was warmer than the usual cool Maine summer evenings, most of the partying was going on outdoors. Carrie could see that the whole backyard of the house was lit up by burning torches.

"Hey, Carrie!" a male voice called to her as she got out of the car after she'd parked it.

Carrie sought out the voice. "Hi, Howie!" she said. It was Howie Lawrence. He was a sweet guy, but Carrie was glad he had a crush on Molly now. He used to have a crush on *her*!

"Great party," Howie commented. "Everyone's here." And then his voice dropped to a whisper. "And I do mean everyone."

"What are you talking about?" Carrie asked.

Howie indicated the back of the house with his head. "Oh, there's a few Hollywood types here. Like Rocky Mountain. Like Duke Underwood. Like Lily Vallez. No sign of the director, though. Emma and Sam are here, too. Want me to show you where they are?"

Carrie nodded, and Howie took the lead as they snaked their way through a huge crowd of kids. Carrie saw something that caught her eye.

"Wait a sec, Howie!" she called, raising her voice to carry over the loud Beatles music that was playing. She quickly grabbed one of her cameras from around her neck, aimed, and fired.

"Got it!" she said to herself. She had caught the pro wrestler Rocky Mountain, standing with his arms out at his sides as if he were a gymnast doing an "iron cross" maneuver, while two kids were doing pull-ups on his arms.

"Wow!" Howie marveled. "Can you believe how strong that guy is?"

"He's nuts," Carrie commented. "Who'd want to spend that much time in the gym!"

"Girlfriend!" Carrie heard Sam's voice calling to her. "I understand you're going to be a star!"

Sam and Emma approached her and Howie, and they stood in a tight little knot off to the side of the Masons' bricked back patio.

"You guys look great!" Carrie said. Sam had on faded jeans, a denim bustier, and a denim baseball cap covered with faux jewels. Emma wore a cute pink and white spaghetti-strapped sundress with a white denim jacket.

"I agree!" Howie said, grinning widely. "Either of you two want to dance?"

"I just talked to Molly," Sam said, grinning a bit mischievously. "She was looking for you."

"Oh, yeah?" Howie asked, his face lighting up.

"She's in the kitchen," Sam added. "Or was, the last time I looked."

"Excuse me, ladies," Howie said and went off to find Molly.

"The boy is crazed for her," Sam declared.

"She's a really nice girl," Emma said.

"So," Sam said, looking Carrie up and down, "I understand Reginald London wants you in his movie."

"That's right," Carrie said noncommittally, not sure how this conversation was going to go.

"I understand you're going to get killed first," Sam noted.

"That's what he told me," Carrie agreed.

"I am so totally psyched!" Sam screeched.

"You are?" Carrie asked. "You're not mad?"

"Are you kidding?" Sam cried. "Now I have a friend in the business! Everybody knows everything in the movies is contacts!"

"Right," Carrie agreed.

"Connections are everything," Sam said knowingly.

"But today, on the beach—"

"Reginald London is a wanker," Sam said superciliously. "Everyone knows that."

"*I* certainly do," Emma agreed.

"She's the smart one," Sam confided to Carrie, nodding at Emma. "After Reginald kicked that girl off the set just for stating her opinion, Emma decided not to even be in the extras scenes."

Carrie looked over at Emma. "Is that true?"

Emma nodded. "He's such a nasty, power-hungry, egocentric little sexist, don't you think?"

Sam laughed. "God, you sound just like your mother right now, Em—"

"Excuse me," a male voice said to Carrie from behind. "Can I talk to you for a second?"

Carrie turned to see who was speaking to her. It was a guy she'd only seen once before in her life. He was smiling at her broadly. His name was Duke Underwood.

"Uh, sure," Carrie said. "Excuse me,

guys," she said to Emma and Sam, who stood there staring after Carrie with their mouths open.

"Don't catch any flies!" Carrie called teasingly back to her friends. Both Emma and Sam snapped their jaws shut.

Before Carrie turned away, she saw something she didn't like at all.

On the face of both of her very best friends was written sheer, unadulterated jealousy.

SEVEN

Carrie's alarm clock woke her up at seven-thirty the next morning, and she wearily got out of bed and made her way to the bathroom.

Home at two A.M. and awake again at seven-thirty. Killer pace, Carrie thought to herself as she dragged herself out of bed. *Gotta get some sleep along the way, here. But when? Great party, anyway, even though Sam seemed as if she was about to give birth when Duke Underwood pulled me aside to talk about a possible photo op later in the week. Enough of this show-biz stuff. I'm glad Billy gets back from Boston tonight.*

Carrie showered and dressed quickly in jeans and a T-shirt, then hustled downstairs. She knew she had a major day's work ahead of her. Not only was she supposed to take Ian and Chloe to the country club in the late morning, but Ian was having another band practice in the afternoon, which Carrie was supposed to chaperone. Then Claudia and Graham were having guests for dinner, and Claudia wanted Carrie to help serve.

Carrie heard loud female voices arguing as she hit the bottom of the stairs.

"Is that why you came here?" Claudia was yelling. "For that?"

"No," Cindi remonstrated. "It's just that—"

I don't think I'd better go in there yet, Carrie decided. She sat down on the bottom step. Claudia's and Cindi's voices carried to where she sat.

"I can't believe this is the reason you

called me!" Claudia interrupted her.

"It's *not* the only reason," Cindi replied defensively.

"Oh, really?" Claudia asked in a cool voice. "I don't recall hearing from you for the last five years."

"I can't help it," Cindi said. "There's no one else!"

"You're doing this because you think I can afford it, that's the only reason," Claudia said in a biting tone.

Doing what? Carrie wondered. She got up to go back upstairs because she felt funny eavesdropping on a private conversation, but what Cindi said next stopped her in her tracks.

"Claudia, he kicked me out of the house!" Cindi cried. "My own daughter said she wanted me to go! Don't you realize that I'm helpless?"

"Oh, Cindi, you've never been helpless in your life," Claudia scoffed.

"You don't know what it's been like for me—"

"No, I don't," Claudia agreed. "You haven't actually made a huge effort to stay in touch with me. But now that you need money, all of a sudden I'm your best friend again!"

"But fifteen thousand dollars is nothing to you!" Cindi pointed out. "And it would save my life!"

"Cindi, aren't you being just a little melodramatic?" Claudia queried.

"Just till I get back on my feet—I've got major debts—"

"And you have the nerve to tell me that you came to see me! You came for money! What about alimony? Don't you have any savings?" Claudia asked.

"Not really—"

"Well," Claudia said, "I really do not think this is fair, your coming to me—"

"But we were best friends!" Cindi cried. "We agreed we would do anything for each other. Anytime! We said that even if we didn't see each other for a long time, our hearts would always be together!"

"That was then," Claudia replied tersely. "This is now. I've barely seen you!"

"That wasn't my call," Cindi shot back.

"What do you mean?" Claudia replied, her voice cracking.

"I mean, I tried!" Cindi responded. "But after you married Graham, you just started pushing me away!"

"I did not!"

"You did too!" Cindi shot back. "When you first started at Polimar, I used to come to New York all the time to see you, and you used to come out to California to see me. We were best buddies. But then you married him, and all of a sudden your friend Cindi Etherdige wasn't good enough for you anymore."

"That's not true—"

"It *is* true," Cindi insisted. "How many times did you call me after you got married. Three? Four? In six years? I sure called you. And got your answering machine instead!"

"I've been busy," Claudia replied, and to Carrie she sounded guilty and defensive.

107

"Busy being the wife of a rich, famous rock star," Cindi replied. "You can get as indignant as you want, Claudia, but you're the one who changed, not me."

There was silence in the kitchen.

"Everyone changes," Claudia finally said. "Everything changes."

"Sure," Cindi said bitterly. "Look, how about ten thousand? That would help."

"Cindi, I'm calling you a cab to take you to the ferry. Go pack your stuff. I really think you should leave."

"Fine," Cindi replied, hurt coloring her voice. "I'll go. But just a few words of advice first. You can lie to me, but don't lie to yourself. You dropped me, not the other way around. So your wounded act just doesn't cut it."

"Cindi, I—"

"Forget it," Cindi replied. "Forget all about me. Oh, that's right—you already did."

Cindi came flying out of the kitchen and ran over to the stairs. Carrie stood up quickly, her face burning with embarrassment for listening in, but Cindi seemed too distraught to even notice. She ran right by Carrie and up to her room, then slammed the door.

Where are the kids? Carrie thought suddenly. *Thank goodness they must still be asleep. That was the ugliest thing I've ever heard in my life. And I don't know who's right or wrong. I don't think Cindi should be asking for money, but maybe she needs it. I don't think Claudia should be sending her old best friend away, but maybe they have grown apart.*

Carrie went back upstairs to her room. She didn't come down again until after she saw the Sunset Island Taxi Company cab arrive and watched Cindi get into it, carrying her duffel bag.

That is so sad, Carrie thought as she watched from the window. *That will never, ever happen with me and Sam and Emma. Never.*

* * *

"Hi," Carrie said carefully when she walked into the kitchen. Claudia was setting breakfast out for Ian and Chloe, who still hadn't awakened.

Claudia greeted Carrie brightly, as if nothing at all had happened.

"Hi, Carrie, good morning!" Claudia said cheerfully. "What a beautiful Maine day!"

"Hi, Claudia," Carrie said, deciding to play it totally cool and not let on that she had overheard the whole blowout argument between Claudia and Cindi. "Where are the kids?"

"Sleeping late," Claudia reported. "We were up playing Nintendo until almost eleven."

"I was out later than that," Carrie admitted.

"We gathered," Claudia said evenly. "Your own time is your own time, Carrie, as long as it doesn't affect your performance on the job."

"Okay," Carrie said, not knowing whether there was a hidden message in Claudia's words or not. She poured herself some coffee and took an English muffin off one of the plates that had been set out on the table.

"Cindi left this morning," Claudia announced, sitting down at the table with Carrie. "She got a call last night about how she's supposed to cover the Sotheby's auction this weekend in New York. So she had to leave."

Liar, Carrie thought, stirring milk into her coffee. *What a terrible time to have to ask about permission to do the film tomorrow. Here goes nothing.*

"Claudia," Carrie said, "I need to talk to you about something."

Carrie saw a guarded look cross Claudia's face.

She thinks I'm going to call her on her fight this morning with Cindi.

"I got asked to be in the movie," Carrie said quickly.

"You what?" Claudia replied, completely

111

unprepared for what Carrie was talking about.

"The movie," Carrie replied. "You know— *Sunset Beach Slaughter*. The director wants me to be in it," Carrie continued. Then she told Claudia the story of how she'd run into Reginald London on the beach, and how he'd offered her the role.

"Well," Claudia said, buttering an English muffin of her own and contemplatively taking a bite. "It sounds exciting. I suppose it'll be okay."

"Great!" Carrie cried, hugely relieved.

"But it seems to me you've been kind of taking advantage of how easygoing we are," Claudia continued.

"What do you mean?" Carrie said, concerned.

"I mean I don't like to feel as if people are taking advantage of me," Claudia said in a steely voice. "Meaning that you work for us, and that's the reason you're here. Not to party or hang out with your friends or be in movies!"

At first Carrie was so completely taken aback that she just sat there. *Why, she's really upset about Cindi,* Carrie realized. *She thought Cindi was taking advantage of her, and she's taking it out on me!*

"Claudia," Carrie said earnestly, "I'm really sorry if you think I've been taking advantage of you and Graham. But this is an unusual circumstance and I . . . I think I do a good job with the kids," she added, determined to stick up for herself.

"You do," Claudia admitted. "You're great with them, Carrie. I'm just making sure your priorities are clear."

"They're clear," Carrie replied firmly.

"So what's the schedule on this movie?" Claudia asked, setting a basket of muffins on the table for the kids.

"We shoot the first scene at the crack of dawn tomorrow morning," Carrie reported. "I was told it would just take an hour or so."

"I suppose that'll be okay," Claudia responded. "Can you be back here by ten to take the kids to the pool?"

"Absolutely," Carrie promised.

"Then we'll see you on the silver screen," Claudia said ironically. "And don't tell Ian. He'll be sure to start throwing demo tapes at you."

"I'll keep that in mind," Carrie said with a smile. "Excuse me." Carrie pulled the business card Reginald London had given her and went to use the phone in the den. An assistant answered the phone.

"Wear a bathing suit," a harried assistant told her when she explained who she was. "Bring a few so we can choose."

"Okay," Carrie agreed nervously. "My bathing suits aren't . . . skimpy or anything," she warned the assistant.

"Oh, God," the assistant groaned. "Well, we'll have to have some others there for you, just in case. What size do you wear?"

"Ten or twelve," Carrie replied, gulping hard. "But I'm not really comfortable in, uh, skimpy things."

"Look, Carol—"

"Carrie," she corrected the assistant.

"Whatever. You are not playing you, who doesn't like skimpy things. You are an actress, and you dress the way the character would dress. Got it?"

"Got it," Carrie answered.

When she hung up, she put her head in her hands. *What have I gotten myself into?*

"So you just press this button, cast it out, and reel it back in as fast as you can," Billy said to Carrie, handing her the spin-casting fishing rod and reel.

"Like this?" Carrie asked doubtfully, checking her balance on the breakwater before letting a feeble cast fly into the ocean.

"Kinda," Billy said, steadying her with his arm. "It takes practice. About five minutes' worth."

It was early evening that same day—Billy had returned from his band-related trip to Boston, and Carrie had actually made it through all the work she had to do. Now she and Billy were out fishing on one of the breakwaters near the main pier. It was a calm evening, and the sometimes turbulent ocean was emerald-green and as calm as glass.

God, was Chloe cranky today, Carrie thought with a sigh as she tried casting the fishing rod again. *Maybe she can sense that things aren't really right with her mother. That was a weird scene this morning. Really weird.*

"That's better," Billy approved, watching Carrie cast.

"So what are we going to catch here, O Great White Hunter?" Carrie teased Billy. "I didn't know that you were such a fisherman."

"Pres's fault," Billy said simply, his face absolutely gorgeous in the soft light of the sunset. "He got me into it. Calms me down. Anyway, we're trying to catch snapper blues."

"Snapper what?"

"Blues," Billy repeated. "Little bluefish,

116

maybe a foot long. They put up a good fight and taste pretty good, too." He took the rod from Carrie and threw the small metal lure out into the ocean. He reeled as hard as he could, but there was no bite.

"Fish not too cooperative, huh?" Carrie joked, readjusting the camera that was slung around her neck and which she never went anywhere without these days. "It's beautiful here now, anyway."

"Not as beautiful as you are," Billy said softly.

"Ha!" Carrie laughed. "Flattery will get you everywhere."

"Imagine—Carrie Alden, movie star!"

"Aw, come on, it's not that big a deal," Carrie protested. She'd told Billy earlier in the evening about how Reginald London III had wanted her to play the part of Luce Kittyn, and Billy had reacted with enthusiasm.

"Hey, it could help the photo shoot," Billy suggested. "Give you another perspective on things."

"I thought of that," Carrie reflected, watching Billy methodically cast and retrieve line.

"Just don't get too much fake blood on your lens," Billy cracked. "I hear you can't wash it off."

"We'll see." Carrie smiled, pressing up against her boyfriend. Billy put his fishing rod down, put his arm around Carrie, and kissed her gently on the lips. Carrie closed her eyes and enjoyed the moment.

Ah, this is perfection, Carrie thought. *Soft evening breeze, no one around, Billy Sampson, and me. Please let this moment never end.*

When Carrie opened her eyes again, she could see that she and Billy were not alone on the breakwater.

"Wait a sec," she said to Billy in an excited voice. She broke out of his embrace and fumbled with her camera equipment.

"What?" Billy asked, completely per-plexed.

"Wow, this could be great," Carrie said under her breath, ignoring Billy. She got up and moved behind the dune. Billy tried to come with her, but Carrie hissed at him to stay right where he was. He did.

A couple was coming toward the spot where Carrie was hidden. It was Rocky Mountain. He was holding hands with Lily Vallez. Rocky Mountain, as everyone knew, was married to the female pro wrestler Penny Dreadful.

"Evenin'," Rocky said to Billy as he and Lily passed by.

Billy nodded his head and continued to fish, a scowl on his face.

When Rocky and Lily had passed by, Carrie came out from behind the dune.

"Got 'em!" she said triumphantly. "Perfect for the photoessay."

"You're kidding," Billy said.

"No," Carrie answered, "I'm not."

"You stopped kissing *me* so that you could take a hidden photo of *them*?" Billy asked Carrie, an ironic smile on his face showing that he really wasn't too mad.

"Always on the job," Carrie replied gaily, snuggling up next to Billy again.

"God, you're as bad as me with the band," Billy replied ruefully, shaking his head.

"Well, we both love our work," Carrie said lightly, snaking her arms around his neck.

A distracted look crossed her face.

"What now?" Billy asked.

"Oh, it just occurred to me that I really shouldn't use that shot—I mean, it was a private moment."

Billy smiled. "Gorgeous *and* ethical," he pronounced.

He kissed Carrie again, and Carrie gave herself up to kissing him back.

And tried not to think about how skimpy a bathing suit she might be asked to wear in Reginald London III's "masterpiece."

EIGHT

Carrie, Duke Underwood, and Rocky Mountain were all huddled together in the dawn chill, steaming cups of coffee in their hands, listening to Reginald London give them a discourse on what he called the "tone-setting" scene—the murder of Carrie on the beach by Rocky.

It was the next morning, and Carrie had woken up at five in order to make it to the beach by six as Reginald had required. First she'd spent a humiliating hour in the wardrobe trailer with an assistant named Marsha. Marsha informed Carrie right away that she was really an actress and that she wasn't in this movie because it "wasn't up to her standards." She looked over Carrie's bathing suits and rolled her eyes, then handed Carrie a white bikini with a teeny-tiny top.

"That?" Carrie asked, totally aghast.

"That," Marsha replied, seeming to enjoy Carrie's dismay.

"B-but I can't," Carrie stammered, staring in horror at the top to the bathing suit. "I mean, I'm too—"

"I'll decide if you're 'too,uh,' " Marsha said superciliously. "Put it on."

Carrie sighed and went behind a curtain to put on the bathing suit. She could just barely get the bottom half on, and when she put on the top her breasts popped right out.

"Excuse me," she called to Marsha, sticking her head out of the curtain. "This is totally impossible. What else have you got?"

Marsha grabbed the curtain away from

Carrie's hand and stared at Carrie, who blushed furiously. "I see your point," Marsha said dryly. "Just a sec."

I am about ten seconds from walking out on this whole thing, Carrie thought to herself as she huddled miserably in the dressing room. *If I didn't need the money so badly for school, I'd be out of here already. . . .*

"Okay, try this," Marsha said, handing Carrie a red two-piece bathing suit.

Thankfully the bottom was more fully cut, and the top had a built-in bra, Carrie realized as she put the suit on. She studied herself in the mirror. *This is sexier than any suit I ever wore in my life,* Carrie realized. She turned back and forth and studied her reflection. *I can't decide if I look like an idiot or if I look cute.* She took a deep breath and opened the curtain. Marsha was sorting some costumes on a rack.

"Is this okay?" Carrie asked uncertainly.

"It'll do," Marsha said grudgingly. "Just be sure to suck in your stomach," she added maliciously.

Suck in my stomach! Carrie thought anxiously. *Oh, no! I look fat! I know I look fat! Imagine how fat I'll look twenty feet tall!*

"Wow, I don't know who you are, but I'd sure like to know," a male extra said, getting a look at Carrie as he stepped into the trailer.

Carrie smiled at him gratefully. *Maybe Marsha is just being nasty. I hope!*

She left the costume trailer and then spent an hour in the hair and makeup trailer. Having her hair done was fun (they set it on hot rollers, and when they brushed it out, she looked like one of those shampoo ads). The makeup part was icky. A thin young man put ten tons of makeup on Carrie's face.

"Why would I be wearing all this makeup on the beach?" Carrie asked him.

He just rolled his eyes and piled on another layer of blush.

When her hair and makeup were done, someone handed Carrie a big velour robe to put on, and then rushed her out into the 55 degree—it had turned cooler over-night—early morning for her meeting with Duke, Rocky, and Reginald.

"Are you ready for this, Carrie?" Reginald asked her, looking at her closely.

"I guess so," Carrie replied, pulling the robe tighter around herself.

"You must know so," Reginald said. "This scene will make or break my movie!"

"I'll do the best I can," Carrie said honestly.

"You'll do fine," Duke assured her.

"I won't mess you up too bad," Rocky offered.

Mess me up? Yikes!

"Okay, let's go over the action again," Reginald said in a preachy tone of voice. "Luce, you've got no lines here. We're going to use a music-over. You and your boyfriend Chaz—Duke, that is—have just spent a passionate night on the beach."

Reginald pointed to a couple of zipped-together sleeping bags that were a ways down the beach, between some camera equipment. Carrie nodded that she understood.

"You, Luce, get the idea that you want to go take an early morning swim. You emerge from the bag, stretch out to the sun, turn, and run to the ocean. Jump in, splash around, you know," Reginald said, a far-off look in his eyes. "Got it?"

"You mean I was sleeping in a bathing suit?" Carrie asked dubiously.

"Of course not!" Reginald exclaimed. "Didn't I tell you we're going for realism? We see you pop out of the bag, your naked breasts gleaming in the morning sunrise—"

"Hold it, hold it, hold it!" Carrie yelled. "Wrong."

"Wrong?" Reginald asked, his eyebrows raised.

"Wrong," Carrie said firmly. "No naked breasts."

"A quick shot of naked buttock, perhaps?" Reginald asked hopefully.

"No naked anything," Carrie said. "If you

want to replace me, that's fine. But I'm not taking off this bathing suit."

Reginald stared hard at Carrie. She could feel the five thousand dollars slipping away. "I knew you were the right girl!" he finally cried.

"I am?"

"Of course!" Reginald rejoiced. "You have integrity! There is so little integrity in art these days. So, you'll have fallen asleep in your bathing suit. Actually, I think it sends a better message," the director mused, nodding. "This is a complex girl, a girl who doesn't give her love so freely—"

"Right," Carrie agreed.

"Besides, I can get the next babe who dies to go full frontal on the nudity," Reginald decided. "The contrast will be brilliant."

"Brilliant," an assistant standing next to Reginald echoed reverently.

"All right, my angel," Reginald said, giving Carrie a little hug. "Are you ready to run, run, run into the ocean?"

"That's it?" Carrie asked dubiously. "What about the murder?"

"We'll do that later," Reginald replied. "I'll want to move the cameras in for close-ups. Lots of close-ups. Lots and lots of close-ups.

"So what are you waiting for?" he continued. "Let's create some art here!" He strode off to his director's chair.

"He's lucky his dad runs the studio," Rocky commented. "Or else I'd pulverize the snot-nosed little cretin."

"He's an *artiste*," Duke said, grinning widely at Carrie. Carrie smiled back. "So—shall we go do this?"

Carrie and Duke walked together to the area where the sleeping bags had been set up. They climbed in together.

"Okay, actors, give me passion!"

Carrie stared at Duke. "I thought this scene began after the kissing part was already over."

Duke shrugged and smiled. "You mind having me kiss you?"

I must be crazy, Carrie thought. *A million girls in America would kill to do a love scene with Duke Underwood.*

"I guess I can handle it," Carrie replied, smiling back at Duke.

Duke put his arms around Carrie and began to kiss her passionately.

"Okey-dokey, this one's for the books. Roll 'em!"

Duke began kissing Carrie again. And she liked it. A lot. Still, a part of her mind was outside herself watching the whole scene.

"Cut! Cut! Cut!"

Reginald's voice rang out from the megaphone.

"What do you think this is, Carrie, *Sesame Street?* You and Chaz are supposed to be teen lovers who just spent a passionate night together. Now, give me some passion! We're talking tongue! Hold a moment, please!"

The director began consulting with an assistant.

A makeup person ran over to Carrie and powdered her face quickly. Duke's private makeup person fixed his hair.

"You got a boyfriend?" Duke asked Carrie as they lay in the sleeping bags, Carrie feeling more uncomfortable then she'd ever been in her life.

"Yes," Carrie admitted. "And I feel pretty strange about all this."

"What's his name?"

"Billy."

"This time," Duke suggested, "try saying his name over and over again during our clinch. The mikes are off, and it might make things easier for you."

Carrie nodded doubtfully.

"Okay, actors, ready and . . . action!"

Carrie and Duke went back to writhing around passionately. This time Carrie did what Duke had suggested, saying Billy's name over and over again. And it seemed to help. She even managed to give Duke a passionate-looking kiss at the end, and then nibbled on his ear.

"Get out of the bag!" Duke hissed to her. "Run to the water!"

Oh, crap, I forgot to do that, Carrie thought.

Carrie climbed out of the bag, fell to her knees and kissed Duke again, and then stretched luxuriously—or about as luxuriously as she could, considering how nervous she was. Then she turned and ran toward the water, and dived in.

"Cut! Cut! Cut! That's better, Carrie, but we're gonna have to do it again. There's a *Je ne sais quoi* that I'm looking for but I'm not seeing."

Reginald consulted his assistant again, nodding eagerly.

"I've got it! Carrie, act like you've just lost your virginity and you are now as free as a bird!"

I just lost my virginity while wearing a bathing suit? And I'm free as a bird? Is he kidding? The morning after I lost my virginity, I remember walking around in a fog, wondering if I'd done the right thing!

131

"I'll try, Reginald," Carrie called gamely.

So this is acting? I think I'll be sticking to photography. It's too bad Sam didn't get this so that she could see that the reality of it isn't like in the movies!

"Go dry off and we'll do it again."

"Dry off?" Carrie asked Reginald. "But where?"

Reginald pointed to a seven-foot-high hot-air fan that had been carted onto the beach by some of the production aides. Carrie went over to it dubiously, but Reginald was right—it was like a giant blow-dryer, and Carrie was completely dry within three minutes. Then fifteen minutes were spent fixing her hair and makeup again. It was incredibly tedious.

Reginald then had Carrie do four or five more takes of the scene with Duke, from the beginning. Each time she had to dry off and get her hair and makeup done again. Finally he pronounced himself satisfied with his footage.

Frankly, I can't tell any difference between one take and another. I feel awful in all of them. Carrie glanced at an assistant's watch: 9:45. *I barely have enough time to make it back home by ten like I promised Claudia.*

"Okay, let's set up Luce's death scene. Everyone ready?"

"Uh, excuse me, Reginald?" Carrie called to him. "You told me this was only going to take an hour."

"And?" Reginald asked.

"And I have to be at my job in fifteen minutes."

Reginald stared down at Carrie. "If you leave you will cost this production many thousands of dollars. Do you think you're worth many thousands of dollars?"

"Well, no, but—"

"Then the matter is settled," Reginald said. "Let's set up the shot."

All the camera people, who had been moving their equipment down to the actual shoreline itself, nodded to Reginald.

"I'm ready," Rocky Mountain reported. He'd changed into an all-white cook's uniform, complete with white hat. In his right hand he held a super-long kitchen knife—it had to be two feet long!—that looked dangerously real to Carrie.

"Here's your blood capsule," an assistant told Carrie, handing her something that looked like a red bullet. "Palm it in your hand so it doesn't show, then when he kills you, just lift your hand to your neck and squeeze—you'll be a bloody mess."

Carrie took the red capsule gingerly. *I hate show business,* she decided. *And please make this scene go quickly or I am in major trouble with Claudia.*

"Okay, Luce, back into the ocean, swim around in bliss, then, come out of the ocean, walk sexy back to Duke. Call out 'Chaz, honey!' Rocky will grab you from behind. When he does, scream that gorgeous scream of yours. Then he'll cut your throat, do the blood thing, fall, that's it. Got it? Good! Okay . . . and action!"

When Reginald called action, Carrie ran into the ocean and did what the director called for. Dripping wet, she emerged and tried to walk as sexily as she could back up the beach—it was a little distracting to have three movie cameras rolling away as she walked, and a boom mike following her all the way. She called out "Chaz, honey," feeling like a total idiot.

It was a complete shock to her when she felt two enormous arms grab her and sweep her off her feet, even though she knew that Rocky Mountain was supposed to assault her.

Carrie screamed involuntarily. Really loud. Rocky held his knife up to the morning sun, where it glistened and glinted as if he had been up all night polishing it. Then he ceremoniously drew it across Carrie's throat.

"*Cut!* Am I a genius or am I a genius? Did you hear that scream?"

"You're a genius, Reginald," a knockout blond female production assistant who looked to be in her early twenties said to Reginald.

"What a scream! An all-time scream. Just what I wanted. You sure we got the scream?"

Reginald looked anxiously over at his sound engineer, who emphatically nodded his head up and down. The sound man was grinning as broadly as Reginald.

"Brilliant, actors! Simply brilliant! Marvelous on the very first take!"

Great, Carrie thought, now that her heart had finally slowed to a normal pace. She looked at her watch. It was ten-fifteen.

"Am I free to go now?" she asked Reginald.

"Just about," Reginald said. He'd climbed down from his flatbed truck perch and was standing next to Carrie. "There's one thing I'd like to do first."

Uh-oh.

"What's that?" Carrie asked him.

"I'd like some footage of you and Duke kissing. You know, standing on the beach, kissing each other hungrily, that sort of thing," Reginald said. "Don't plan to use it now, but you never know."

"But I'm so late—" Carrie protested.

Reginald flipped some hair off his forehead. "You seem to be under the impression that my film revolves around your schedule."

"No, but—"

"But I think you can manage to squeeze in a few little kisses before you trot off to where you're going to trot off," Reginald said in a frosty voice.

"Okay," Carrie said with a sigh.

"So go dry off again," Reginald instructed her, "and bring yourself over to that camera set up by the boardwalk."

Carrie glanced at her watch again.

"Don't worry," Reginald said, catching her checking the time. "This won't take five minutes."

Carrie sat in a chair while the makeup and hair people fussed over her. That alone took another fifteen minutes. Finally she was ready. She walked over to the board-walk and stood by Duke. Five different cameras surrounded them, and a boom mike hung overhead. Reginald had reassumed his perch up on the truck.

"Okay, actors! Lots of kissing, lots of passion, you are the two hottest kids on Sunset Island, and here's your chance to prove it!"

Duke looked at Carrie and smiled wryly. "What do you think of the movies?" he asked.

"I'm glad I'm at Yale," Carrie responded with a grin.

"Okay, lights, camera, and action!"

Duke and Carrie immediately embraced and began kissing each other. Carrie felt the heat of the lights on their faces. She tried to muster as much enthusiasm as she could for being in Duke Underwood's arms, but between the cameras and the hot lights, and her anxiety over being late for work, it could have been any stranger in the world.

"Okay! It's a wrap! Thank you, Duke. Thank you, Carrie, thank you Rocky. Crew, set up the second beach death scene."

Carrie sighed a big sigh of relief. *It's over. Well, I did make five thousand dollars. I just hope I still have a job.*

She hurried toward the trailer to change her clothes, and saw a familiar silhouette standing on the other side the trailer.

It was Billy. She started to run to him, but then stopped dead in her tracks. A huge knot of anxiety formed in her stomach.

She had never seen anyone look so angry in her entire life.

NINE

"You actually expect me to believe that?" Billy asked Carrie.

She'd walked over to him and tried to kiss him, but he'd turned away. As late as she was, she couldn't stand to leave Billy without assuring him that she hadn't particularly enjoyed kissing Duke Underwood.

Well, I did enjoy it at first, Carrie admitted to herself. *I mean, what girl wouldn't? But then it just got to be work. . . .*

"Come on, Billy," Carrie pleaded with him, "I'm running late and this isn't fair!"

"It isn't?" Billy said, a hard look on his

face. "What am I supposed to think? No way you didn't enjoy kissing him, Carrie. It looked to me like you were enjoying it a lot."

"Well, I wasn't," Carrie said flatly. She was beginning to feel irritated. "Look, I'm incredibly late and I have to get back or I might not have a job. So can we just wait on this for a while?"

"Sure, we can wait," Billy said in a cold voice.

Carrie reached out and touched Billy's arms. "This isn't like you."

"Maybe it's exactly like me," Billy said.

"Billy," Carrie said softly, "there are girls all over you all the time when you guys play a gig. You flirt with them when you sing—it's part of your job! I don't believe you want them instead of me."

Billy sighed. "Good point," he mumbled.

"Look, I've absolutely got to go or I am in big trouble," Carrie said. "Call me?"

"How 'bout I stop by the house tonight to see you?"

"Make it tomorrow night and you got it," Carrie said, fumbling in her purse for her keys. "I'm exhausted and tonight all I want to do is go to sleep."

"Okay, but . . . all right, I'll see you then!" Billy kissed Carrie quickly, and then Carrie dashed for the Templetons' car.

What am I going to tell Claudia and Graham? she thought guiltily as she drove back to the house. *Claudia is going to kill me!*

"Carrie, fax for you!" Ian Templeton sang out as Carrie ran through the front door.

"Thanks, Ian," Carrie said, her voice a little hoarse from screaming.

I wonder who'd be sending me a fax? Carrie asked herself as she took the single sheet of paper from Ian. It was on Westwood Studios stationery:

To: Carrie Alden
From: Monika McLaughlin,
Production Assistant
Re: Sunset Beach Slaughter
Carrie:

Reginald has asked me to send this to you to tell you that he is planning to shoot the early scene where you waitress at the Slay Café tomorrow beginning at 5:30 A.M. Location just outside the Play Café. Also, he loves your scream and wants to hear it echo off buildings. We will send a limo for you tomorrow. Thank you very much. We are counting on you.

I can't believe this is happening to me, Carrie thought. *Up this morning at five, now a full day with the kids, and I've got to do it again tomorrow? And how the hell am I supposed to get Claudia to go along with this little missive?*

"You're late," Ian said, grinning a little.

"That's true," Carrie admitted, flopping into a chair. "Where are your folks?"

"They left an hour ago," Ian replied. "Mom said you were already late—"

"Oh, no—" Carrie groaned.

"—but she was sure you'd be here any

143

minute," Ian continued. "So she doesn't know that you're *this* late."

Carrie gave Ian a pleading look.

"Of course I won't tell!" Ian exclaimed. "You're a movie star now!" He grinned a boyish grin at Carrie. "I would never tell on you, anyway," he added.

Carrie gave him a hug. "You're a sweetheart," she told him. "Where's Chloe?"

"Taking a nap," Ian reported. "Mom let her stay up late again last night. The *Muppet Movie* was on. Hey, now that you're a movie star, would you put in a good word for my song on the soundtrack?"

Carrie laughed. "I'll do what I can, but I don't think I have any clout."

"Of course you do!" Ian insisted.

"Why don't you play me the song," Carrie suggested.

"This afternoon," Ian promised. "I've got to remix it."

"I'm going to check on Chloe," Carrie said, forcing herself out of the comfortable chair.

She went upstairs and found the little girl sound asleep, her favorite stuffed bunny cuddled in her arms.

Carrie stroked the little girl's silky hair, then she lay her head down next to Chloe's on the pillow.

In a moment she was as sound asleep as Chloe.

"So how was it, Carrie?" Ian Templeton asked eagerly as Carrie dragged herself through the doorway of the Templetons' house for the second day in a row after hours of screaming, dying, and kissing—not necessarily in that order.

"Great, just great," Carrie said without enthusiasm. "I've still got fake blood in my hair. Look!"

"Cool!" Ian exclaimed.

"Let me go upstairs and shower, okay?" Carrie said to Ian.

"Sure," Ian replied. "Did you talk to Reginald London about my song?"

Carrie shook her head no. "There was no time."

"We've still got some time," Ian said. "You pick the right opportunity. I'm counting on you. Look, I'll be downstairs working on another new song. Mom's getting ready to leave. Dad's by the pool."

Carrie went up the main stairway to her room and collapsed, exhausted, on her bed. She knew she should hurry. Claudia had agreed to let her spend the morning working on the film for the second day in a row, but Carrie knew her employer had just about had it with her asking for time off. In fact, although she'd listened to Carrie's explanation about why she'd been late the day before (and luckily Claudia had no idea how late she'd really been), she told Carrie it had better not happen again. The implied threat was pretty clear—Carrie's job would be at stake.

Yet as much as she knew she should hussle, she was simply too exhausted to move. She closed her eyes, and a million images raced through her mind, as if she were watching them in sped-up motion on a movie screen.

Being fitted with a too tight, too short waitress's uniform. Carrying platters of food to extras while Rocky Mountain watched her through the kitchen door. Fake blood being squirted on her from head to toe. Reginald London III ordering her to scream, over and over again; and the sound of the scream echoing off the buildings on Main Street. The glare of the movie klieg lights in her eyes as she walked out of the Play Café, now remade into the Slay Café. The feel of Rocky Mountain's muscle-bound arms around her neck. Duke Underwood's friendly kiss good-bye when she finally got to leave.

Finally Carrie got up and dragged herself into the shower. When she was done, she felt a little better—*at least that fake blood is out of my hair!*—but she still felt unbelievably tired. She quickly dressed and headed downstairs, where Ian and Chloe were playing Nintendo.

"Mom and Dad are gone," he told her.

"Are they mad at me?" Carrie asked him.

"Nah, Mom was mad at Dad about something else, so I think she forgot to be mad at you."

"Good," Carrie replied, her voice a little zombielike.

"You okay?" Ian asked with concern.

"More or less," Carrie said with a small grin. "Tired. But I'll make it."

"Good," Ian announced. "Because they aren't going to be back until like nine o'clock tonight. There's dinner for us in the fridge."

It was all Carrie could do to get through the day with Ian and Chloe without falling asleep. She made the mistake of taking them to the club to go swimming— she nearly dozed off while she was supposed to be watching Chloe in the kiddie pool. Then Ian insisted that Carrie play Ping-Pong with him, and Carrie was feeling so guilty about almost falling asleep while watching Chloe, she actually agreed. While Chloe cheered her on, Ian beat her in three straight games, and Carrie ended up feeling more tired than ever. Then, just before they were ready to leave, Chloe started to complain that her stomach was hurting her.

"Where does it hurt?" Carrie asked her, gathering up their towels and other belongings.

"Everywhere," Chloe answered. "I feel sick."

"Do you feel like you're going to throw up?"

"No," Chloe said, "just sick." She lay down on one of the chaise lounges at the club, and Carrie finally had to carry her out to the car for the ride home. And no sooner had they arrived back at the house and started unloading their stuff than Chloe did throw up. A lot.

"Eeeyyouu!" Ian gagged as Chloe was bent over by the walkway to the house, heaving.

Chloe gagged some more.

"Leave your sister alone!" Carrie yelled, starting to lose her composure. "Take this stuff inside."

Fortunately, Ian did what Carrie said, and Carrie went over to help little Chloe.

"I'm sorry," Chloe said, "I didn't mean to be sick."

"It's okay, sweetie," Carrie soothed the little girl, rubbing her back.

Graham and Claudia are not going to be delighted to find vomit on their front walk. Which means that guess who is going to have to clean it up? Me!

"Are you feeling any better now?" Carrie asked Chloe. "Sometimes it helps to get it out."

"A little," Chloe said. "Can you wash me?"

Carrie picked Chloe up, carried her to the upstairs bathroom, wet a washcloth, and wiped the young girl down. Then she checked Chloe's temperature. *Hmm, she doesn't have a fever,* Carrie thought. *Must be a stomach virus.* She helped Chloe put on her nightgown and then tucked her into bed. She was just finishing when the doorbell rang downstairs.

"You try to get some sleep, now, okay?"

Carrie told Chloe as she smoothed the curls back from the little girl's face.

"Okay, Carrie," Chloe said in a small voice.

"Carrie!" Ian's voice carried up the stairs. "Friends for you!"

Carrie walked slowly down the stairs, not even noticing that some of Chloe's mess had ended up on her own T-shirt. Standing at the bottom of the stairs were Emma and Sam, laughing and joking a mile a minute.

"Hi, Carrie," Sam said cheerfully as Carrie approached them. "You look like dogmeat."

"Actually, you look busy," Emma added.

"I am busy." Carrie sighed. "Look, Chloe's sick and has been throwing up and I'm—

"Carrie," Chloe said to her from the top of the stairs, "I need you." Chloe looked really cute in her little pink nightgown.

"She doesn't exactly look sick," Sam offered.

"Trust me," Carrie replied wearily, "she

was. Check out the front walk."

"I was," Chloe piped up. "Carrie taked care of me."

"Carrie takes care of everyone," Emma said gently.

"Except Carrie," Carrie mumbled under her breath.

"What do you mean by that, you big movie star?" Sam joked with her.

"What I mean is that I'm exhausted and I'm not exactly prepared for company," Carrie snapped, losing her temper a little.

"Well, excuuuuuuse us for living," Sam said.

"Hey, Carrie," Emma murmured, "we know you've been working really hard lately."

"True," Carrie answered.

"So we came by to invite you to lunch tomorrow," Emma suggested.

"Yeah, that's right, lunch!" Sam added.

"If I can get free—" Carrie said.

"Taken care of," Sam answered, picking up a can of tennis balls that had been left at the bottom of the stairs and balancing the can in one hand.

"What do you mean?" Carrie asked.

"I mean we called Claudia this morning and demanded that she let you come eat lunch with us," Sam said easily. "Who can resist me?"

"You shouldn't have done that!" Carrie cried, feeling guilty about all the time she'd taken off. "She's already ticked off at me and—"

"Hey, Sam is kidding," Emma interrupted. "She just asked Claudia and Claudia said it was fine."

"I'm overreacting," Carrie said wearily. She looked down at her shirt and saw a bit of Chloe's vomit. "God, I look so gross—"

"Well, you clean up nice," Sam teased her. "So, listen, tomorrow will be a blast. All the guys'll be there, too."

"Play Café, twelve-thirty tomorrow?" Emma asked.

"Yeah, sure," Carrie said, only half concentrating on the conversation.

"Carrie!" Chloe called downstairs. "I might be feeling sick again!"

"I gotta go," Carrie said, pushing some hair off her face. She turned around and quickly headed for the stairs.

"Oh, no prob, we'll see ourselves out!" Sam called after her.

Guess I wasn't much of a hostess, Carrie thought ruefully as she hurried up to Chloe. *I'll have to explain the whole thing to Sam and Emma tomorrow.* She got a whiff of her own shirt and practically gagged, but she didn't have time to change until she saw if Chloe was okay. The doorbell rang again. "Just hold on a sec, Chloe!" she called to the little girl.

"But I feel icky!" Chloe cried.

Carrie swore under her breath and ran back downstairs again. She pulled open the door.

It was Billy.

"What are you doing here?" she demanded before she could stop herself.

"Nice greeting," Billy said sarcastically.

"We have a date, remember?"

Carrie stared at him blankly.

"Yesterday you told me to come over tonight, and I'm here," Billy said. "These are for you." He unenthusiastically thrust some roses at Carrie.

"God, I'm sorry, Billy," Carrie said, instantly contrite. "Come on in. I'm just beat to hell."

"Carrie!" Chloe yelled from upstairs.

"I've gotta go," Carrie told Billy and took the stairs two at a time.

"You want me to help you into the bathroom?" Carrie asked the white-faced little girl.

"I think maybe I'm better now," Chloe said, lying down on her pillow.

"Good," Carrie said and gently tucked the blankets in around the child.

"Can you stay here in case I get sick again?" Chloe asked worriedly.

"Sure," Carrie said with a sigh. "I just need to go say good-bye to Billy, and then I'll be right back to be with you, okay?"

Carrie ran back down to Billy, who was drumming his fingers impatiently on the coffee table.

"Chloe's sick," Carrie explained. "I've got to go sit with her."

"Meaning I'm leaving?" Billy asked.

Carrie nodded. "I'm sorry. As soon as I get the kids to bed I'm going to sleep. I am whipped."

"You work too hard," Billy said, his attitude softening when he saw how totally exhausted Carrie really was. "Okay, you can blow me off this once," he teased. "But I'll see you tomorrow, right?"

"You're everything," Carrie said softly. "Now kiss me goodbye and let me go."

"You got it," Billy said, and he moved close to her.

The phone rang.

"Put it on the speakerphone," Carrie suggested to Billy. "It's over by the bookcase. I'm too tired to get up."

Billy walked over to the phone and flipped a switch.

"Templeton residence," Carrie said in a loud voice.

"Carrie!" a sort-of-familiar male voice said. "How you doing?"

"Who is this?" Carrie asked, trying to place the voice in her head.

"It's Duke Underwood," the voice said.

"Oh, hi, Duke," Carrie said. She saw a hard look come over Billy's face, and she shrugged an I-don't-know-why-Duke-is-calling-me at her boyfriend.

"Hey, I had fun today," Duke said easily. "You kiss great, by the way."

"I'm outta here," Billy hissed.

"Billy, wait!" Carrie cried.

"Just forget it!" Billy yelled, and he was gone.

"Excuse me?" Duke's voice asked.

"Nothing," Carrie replied, heaving a sigh. "Nothing at all."

"Good," Duke said. "Look, I really called to congratulate you for your hard work this morning. I know it wasn't easy."

Wait a sec, here. Is someone actually

*thanking me for something that I did,
instead of complaining?*

"Thanks, Duke," Carrie said distractedly.
"I'm sorry, my mind's on something else."
She kept seeing the image of Billy storming
out of the living room.

"That's cool, I know you're beat," Duke
replied. "Listen, you did tell me that you
want to make documentary films, didn't
you?"

"Yeah," Carrie agreed, although she had
no idea what that had to do with anything
at all.

"Great!" Duke said. "Well, this friend of
mine is here, and I thought you might like
to meet her—"

"Carrie!" Chloe called down to her. "I feel
sick again!"

"I've got to go," Carrie told Duke quickly.

"Okay, it can wait," Duke said. "I'll call
you in the morning, okay?"

"Fine," Carrie said and hung up.

She hurried back upstairs to Chloe.

At the moment she couldn't care less who

Duke's "friend" might be.

I don't want to hear from one more person tonight, Carrie thought to herself as she rounded the corner to Chloe's room. *Not Sam. Not Emma . . .*

A picture of Billy childishly storming out of the house without even waiting for an explanation filled her head.

And especially not Billy.

TEN

The next morning the sun was shining, the birds were singing, and Carrie felt a hundred thousand percent better.

It's amazing what actually getting some sleep can do for a person's disposition, Carrie thought, smiling as she watched a robin outside her window.

After getting Chloe to sleep (she hadn't been sick again, thank God), Carrie had cleaned up and spent some time with Ian. When she finally got him off to bed, she went to her room, tore off her clothes, and fell into her bed, asleep the instant her head hit the pillow.

She dimly remembered her friends stopping over the day before. *God, I was so out of it I barely remember,* Carrie realized. *Well, I'll make it up to them,* she promised herself, *as soon as I can.*

She heard the phone ring and looked over at the clock on her nightstand. Eight o'clock. Time enough to shower and get downstairs by eight-thirty, Carrie figured, which is the time Claudia was expecting her to start work.

There was a knock on her door. "Carrie, phone for you," Ian said through the door. "I've got the new cordless—want me to bring it in?"

Carrie looked down at herself and realized she'd fallen into bed naked. "Just a sec," she called to him, grabbing an oversize sleeping T-shirt from the foot of her bed. She yanked it on over her head, then said, "Come on in."

Ian handed her the phone. "It's a guy, but it's not Billy," Ian reported.

"Thanks," Carrie said. She could tell

Ian wanted to hang out and listen in, but he reluctantly left the room.

"Hello?"

"Hi, Carrie, it's Duke," came the friendly, sexy voice through the phone.

"Oh, hi," Carrie said, surprised to hear from him.

"So, I told you I'd call you this morning," Duke reminded her.

"Right!" she agreed, even though she'd just that moment recalled that she'd spoken with him at all.

"Have you ever heard of Lina Weller?" Duke asked.

"Lina Weller the documentary film-maker?" Carrie asked.

"That's the one," Duke agreed.

"Are you kidding? I love her films!" Carrie cried. "Did you see the one she did on sexism in grade school? Where teachers graded papers differently if they thought a boy student or a girl student had done the work? And the one that won an Academy Award last year for best documentary, about the black man who was imprisoned for a crime he didn't commit? That was so brilliant!"

"Hey, you don't have to convince me," Duke said with a laugh. "She's a really good friend of mine!"

"No kidding?" Carrie marveled. "Wow, I would love to meet her some time."

"Well, that's what I've been trying to tell you," Duke said. "She's here on the island, hanging out on the set, taking a break before her next film. I thought maybe we could all have lunch together."

"Me have lunch with Lina Weller??" Carrie screeched.

"Well, she eats with a knife and fork just like everybody else," Duke teased.

"I would love to have lunch with her, I would absolutely love to!" Carrie cried.

"Cool," Duke said easily. "The thing is, she mentioned to me that she's looking for an intern for her next film and I thought of you."

Carrie's jaw dropped open. "Me? An

intern for Lina Weller?"

"Yeah, I told her about you and—"

"You *told* her about me?" Carrie yelped.

"Gee, there's an echo on this phone," Duke said. "Yes, I told her about you. So she said she'd like to meet you."

"Why are you being so nice to me?" Carrie asked Duke.

"Hey, contrary to what the tabloids say about me, I'm a reasonably nice guy," Duke joked.

"Seriously," Carrie asked.

"Seriously, then," Duke said. "I have absolutely no ulterior motives. You're in love with what's-his-name, and I'm living with a great girl named Julia. I just like you."

"Wow," Carrie breathed. "I hardly know what to say. Thank you so much!"

"Well, let's see if the two of you hit it off first. How's twelve-thirty at the Slay Café?"

"Terrific," Carrie agreed. "I can't wait!"

"See you," Duke said and hung up.

Unbelievable, Carrie thought as she carried the cordless phone out into the hall. *I am having lunch with one of my great idols of all time. I might even get to work for her!*

"So, who was the guy?" Ian asked, coming up to Carrie.

Carrie laughed. "You are so nosy!"

"Inquisitive," Ian corrected her loftily. "It's a sign of great intelligence."

"Oh, is that so?" Carrie asked. "Well, actually, that was Duke Underwood. He invited me to lunch with—"

"Cool, too cool!" Ian cried. "It's the perfect time to slip him my tape! You've still got it, right?"

"Right," Carrie reluctantly agreed.

"Thanks, Car," Ian said with a huge grin. Before she knew it, he had sped away.

I only hope Ian's song is decent, Carrie thought ruefully as she walked into the hall, *although frankly I'd be shocked if it was. Maybe I should just tell him no. After all, even his dad didn't want to get involved in this and—*

"Good morning," Claudia said, interrupting Carrie's thoughts as Carrie reached the hall. "Listen, you're free this morning," Claudia said. "I'm taking the kids with me to the beach and then we're going out to lunch. But can you be back by two-thirty to take Chloe to see that new Disney movie?"

"Sure," Carrie said eagerly.

"Great," Claudia replied. "I'm sorry if I've been a little hard on you lately. I've . . . had some things on my mind," Claudia added.

"No problem," Carrie told her employer. She practically ran back into her room, filled with glee. The morning off—and lunch with Lina Weller! It was all too perfect!

Carrie decided on taking a leisurely swim in the backyard pool—something she rarely had time to do. Claudia and the kids waved good-bye to her when they left. She waved back and lay down on a chaise lounge, enjoying the warm sun on her skin.

Now if only Billy would call and apolo-

gize, everything would be perfect, Carrie thought. The image of him storming out the night before flitted through her mind again. *It was so unreasonable!* Carrie thought. *It reminds me of something Kurt would do to Emma!*

Carrie went upstairs and treated herself to a long, hot shower, then carefully got ready for her lunch with Duke and Lina. She tried on half of the clothes in her closet before settling on black cotton pants, a black T-shirt and a black and red checked vest. She put on a touch of mascara and some lip gloss, then studied her image in the mirror.

"The question is, do you look like the kind of girl Lina Weller would make her intern?" she asked her reflection.

She glanced at her watch—twelve-fifteen—just time enough to get to the Play Café. At the last minute she grabbed her portfolio, and hoped that bringing it wouldn't look too pushy.

"I'm not nervous, I'm not nervous,"

Carrie chanted to herself as she drove to lunch. She found an empty parking space, parked, and strode briskly toward the restaurant.

Carrie opened the door to the café—it took her a moment for her eyes to adjust to the dimmer light. Then she looked around the crowded room for Duke and Lina.

"Hey, girlfriend!" Sam's familiar voice called to her from across the room.

Carrie looked in that direction. And sitting there at their usual table, under the video monitor, were Sam, Emma, Kurt, Pres, and Billy. They were all smiling and waving to her.

Oh, my God. I was supposed to meet them all for lunch!

"Get a move on, girl!" Pres called to her. "We're starved!"

Carrie's feet were rooted to the floor.

How could I? How could I possibly forget that I was supposed to meet my very best friends and the guy I love?

"Carrie?"

She looked up, and there was Duke Underwood.

"Lina and I are sitting over there." Duke pointed to the far side of the room. "I thought you might not be able to see us in this madhouse."

I want to die. I absolutely want to die.

"Are you okay?" Duke asked, taking Carrie's elbow. "You look kind of white."

"Uh, sure," Carrie said with a weak smile. "Listen, I need to . . . go speak with some friends of mine for a moment. I'll be right over after that."

"Okay," Duke agreed. "But let's not keep Lina waiting."

Carrie nodded and smiled at Duke automatically, then she headed over to her friends' table.

"Hi," Billy said softly. He put his arm out indicating that she should sit in the empty seat next to him.

She sat.

"Are you okay?" Emma asked. "Did you catch Chloe's stomach flu?"

I wish. "No . . ." Carrie began.

Billy let his hand drop down to Carrie's shoulder. He leaned over and nuzzled her ear. "Hey, I'm sorry about last night," he said. "I shouldn't have just walked out like that." Then he kissed her neck softly.

"Uh, listen," Carrie said nervously. "I . . . I . . ." She just couldn't bear to tell them the stupid mistake she'd made.

"How come you're carrying your portfolio?" Sam asked. She looked around the restaurant. "Where's the waitress? I am dying of hunger! Pres, can you flag down that waitress?"

"She'll get here as soon as she can, babe," Pres told her.

"I'll be dead of malnutrition by that time," Sam insisted. She turned back to Carrie. "Hey, I saw you with Duke Underwood at the door. The guy is a total babe."

Carrie attempted a smile.

"Listen, you really don't look well," Emma insisted, staring at Carrie.

Carrie took a deep breath. "Look, I don't

know how to tell all of you this," she began. "I . . . I did something really dumb. Duke called me this morning and invited me to have lunch with him and Lina Weller—she's the greatest documentary filmmaker in the world—and I got so excited about it I . . . I forgot I was supposed to have lunch with all of you."

Everyone started at Carrie.

"You forgot?" Billy finally said.

Carrie nodded. "The reason I have my portfolio is that Lina is looking for an intern for her next film, and she might be considering me. She's waiting for me right now. . . ."

"Wait a sec," Billy said slowly. "You are blowing me off *again?*"

"Oh, no!" Carrie insisted. "I'm not—"

"You mean you didn't come to meet us?" Sam asked.

"I would have," Carrie tried to explain. "I just forgot! Try to understand—"

"Oh, we understand all right," Billy said. "Go off and have lunch with the beautiful people, with *Duke,*" he added maliciously.

"Duke was just trying to do me a favor—" Carrie pleaded.

"I bet," Billy said tersely. "And I can imagine what kind of favors you already did for him."

Carrie stood up abruptly. "That was low, Billy. It's not true and you know it."

Billy just stared at her, his jaw clenched. Carrie looked around the table. No one said a word. Even Emma wouldn't quite look her in the eye.

"Look, I'm really sorry," Carrie told them earnestly. "I know I messed up. I'll make it up to all of you. I promise." The she hurried across the room to Duke and Lina.

"Well, I have to say I love your port-folio," Lina said as she came to Carrie's last shot, taken during a recent hurricane on the island. She tapped a finger against the plastic cover. "This juxtaposition of the power of nature and this poor little boy's face—it's really impressive."

"Thanks," Carrie said, attempting a smile.

Carrie snuck a glance across the room at her friends. She just couldn't help herself. She'd been sitting with Lina and Duke for an hour already—they'd ordered salads, talked about film, and now Lina was actually complimenting Carrie's work—and still she couldn't quite concentrate on anything. She just felt too awful.

She glanced over at Lina. *Why do I feel so disappointed about meeting her?* she wondered. I should be doing cartwheels! *Is she really as obnoxious as she seems, or am I just feeling so guilty that I won't let myself like her?*

"So . . . I gather Duke mentioned to you that I'm interested in finding some new blood to work with me on my next project," Lina said, pushing her straight black hair back carelessly. She was an attractive woman in her late thirties, by Carrie's guess, slender, dressed all in black. Her skin looked coarse and old, though, which

Carrie figured was due to the incredible number of cigarettes she smoked. Carrie had counted six in the past hour.

Lina lit another cigarette and dropped the match in her half-eaten salad. "I demand a lot from my people," Lina continued imperiously. "More than one hundred percent at all times—I mean twenty-four hours a day."

"Oh, I understand completely," Carrie agreed.

Lina exhaled some smoke in Carrie's direction. "Frankly, I'm not sure if you'd be right for me," Lina said.

Carrie was taken a back. "Why is that?"

"Too original," Lina said bluntly.

"But . . . but your work is so original!" Carrie exclaimed.

"Exactly," Lina said with a thin-lipped smile. "My work. My creativity. No one else's."

"I see," Carrie agreed.

"Still, it's a great training ground, if you're really serious about doing docs,"

Lina said, crushing her cigarette out on the floor with the toe of her shoe. "Also, I've discovered some great talent along the way." She smiled over at Duke. "Haven't I, babe?"

Duke smiled back at Lina. "Absolutely," he agreed.

Carrie looked at Duke. "You were in a documentary film?"

"TV commercial," Duke corrected.

"Oh, sweetheart, there's next to no money in docs," Lina said airily. "Even I have to bastardize myself now and then to keep my head above water."

"Well, I think that's a shame," Carrie said sincerely. "I mean, a great artist like you, and you're famous!"

"America does not reward great art, Carrie," Lina said with a shrug. "But I did make heavy six figures last year doing commercials."

"Any dessert here?" the harried waitress asked, clearing off their dirty dishes.

"No, thanks," Carrie said. She snuck a

peek at her watch. It was 2:25. *Let's see,* thought Carrie. *The Disney movie starts at . . . three-fifteen? Yeah, that's right.* So far so good. She should be able to be back by three.

"Espresso," Lina ordered, "and what's fresh-baked back there for dessert?"

"Nothing," the waitress said bluntly. "We order our desserts in from Sweet Sue's, and we're out of just about everything."

Lina laughed. "An honest waitress! I like that! Make it a double espresso, then. Duke?"

"Coffee is fine," Duke said.

"So, Carrie, tell me a bit more about yourself," Lina suggested as she lit up another cigarette.

Some loud laughter caught Carrie's attention. She turned to see her friends clowning around, heading toward the door of the restaurant. For just a moment she caught Billy's eye, and what she saw there made her heart clutch with fear. Then Billy ostentatiously put his arm around

Sam, cracked some joke Carrie couldn't hear, and the group boisterously walked out the door.

"Carrie?" Lina asked.

"Oh, sorry," Carrie said, snapping her head back to her own table. "Well, I've been interested in film and photography forever. . . ." Carrie began.

Lina seemed blasé about everything until Carrie talked about being a student at Yale.

"Really?" Lina asked, clearly impressed. "You know, Yale turned me down years ago. At the time I was cut to the quick."

"Two coffees," the waitress said, putting cups on the table.

"I didn't ask for coffee, I asked for double espresso," Lina said.

"You did?" the waitress asked dully.

"I did."

"Well, I think maybe the espresso machine is broken," the waitress said, obviously trying to get Lina to accept the coffee.

"Young lady," Lina began and proceeded to lecture the exhausted waitress on how to do her job correctly.

Carrie snuck another peek at her watch. Two-forty. If Lina continued to argue and waited for another espresso, Carrie would definitely be late.

"So, please come back with exactly what I ordered," Lina finished.

"Fine," the waitress mumbled and hurried off.

"Excellence in all things, that's my motto, right, Duke?" Lina asked with a smile. She gave his hand a squeeze.

"Right," Duke agreed, sipping his coffee.

"Listen, I'm really sorry to do this, but I have to get back to my job," Carrie blurted out.

Lina raised her eyebrows at Carrie.

"Excellence in all things," Carrie quoted Lina, getting up with a shrug. "Right now I'm trying to apply that to getting back to my job when I said I would."

Lina looked at Duke. "Duke, you didn't

mention your friend had a job. I thought she was an actress."

"Well, she is—I mean, was," Duke said with a laugh. "It's kind of hard to explain. . . ."

"Believe me, my being in this movie with Duke is a total fluke," Carrie said, picking up her purse and her portfolio.

"So, what do you do?" Lina asked, lighting yet another cigarette.

"I'm an au pair," Carrie explained.

"A babysitter?" Lina asked, surprised.

"Yes, and right now an about-to-be-late one," Carrie added. "Thank you so much for lunch, and it was just terrific meeting you." Carrie shook hands with Lina.

"I like your style, Carrie," Lina said.

"I'll walk you to the door," Duke offered.

When they were out of Lina's earshot, Carrie asked him, "Did I do okay?"

"You were terrif," Duke assured her. "Don't mind Lina—she comes on kind of strong, but she's really great."

"Listen, thanks again for this—"

"No prob," Duke said, leaning over to kiss Carrie's cheek. "Hey, what was your boyfriend's name again?"

"Billy," Carrie replied, taken aback.

"Billy," Duke repeated, nodding. He leaned close and whispered into Carrie's ear. "Well, it was a pleasure standing in for ole Billy in those kissing scenes, Carrie, and that's the truth."

Before Carrie could begin to think up a response, Duke gave her a mischievous grin and walked away.

ELEVEN

Just made it!

Carrie pulled into the Templeton's driveway after lunch just after the deejay on WBLM announced the time at 2:55 and promised a set of eight nonstop songs coming right up.

If we hustle, we can still make the movie, Carrie thought, *so long as Chloe's dressed.* Even as she had that thought, she could see Chloe dressed up in one of her pretty flowered outfits, waiting anxiously by the front door.

Carrie stopped the car and bounded out. *Not that I'm all that up to see* Pinocchio *again, but I know that this kid is going to love it.*

"Ready for the movie?" Carrie sang out as she came in the front door.

Chloe stood there silently. Then she burst into tears.

"What's wrong?" Carrie said, her voice full of concern. *Oh no, I hope she doesn't have a relapse of her stomach virus and puke all over me again.*

Chloe sobbed and sobbed. "You're late," she finally mumbled in between gulps for air. "We missed it."

"No, we didn't," Carrie said reasonably, "your mom told me that it starts at three-fifteen. We can still make it."

"Uh-uh," Chloe said. "We're missing it."

"Where's your mother?" Carrie asked.

"On the phone," Chloe sobbed, tears rolling down her face and onto her flower-print dress. "Back there." She indicated the kitchen.

"Newspaper around?" Carrie asked. Then she spotted the latest issue of the *Breakers* right by the front hall steps. She turned to the movie listings for Sunset Island and Portland, completely confident that she'd find that the Sunset Cinema matinee started at three-fifteen.

There it is! she thought triumphantly, her eyes finding the listing for Sunset Cinema.

Then her heart sank.

The movie listings said 2:45, 5:00, and 7:30. There was no 3:15 show.

She's right. I'm wrong. Again, Carrie thought. *I totally screwed up again. What can I say to her?*

Carrie turned and faced the weeping child.

"Chloe," she said gently, "I made a mistake. A big mistake, I'm sorry."

Chloe nodded a little.

"I'll try to get your mom to let me take you to one of the other shows today, okay?" Carrie asked.

Chloe nodded again. "My mommy wants to talk to you, I think," she said, wiping her eyes with the back of her hand.

"I'm sure," Carrie said grimly.

I am about to get slaughtered, and I deserve it, she thought miserably. *How could I have fouled this up?*

"I'll go and—" Carrie began, but she was interrupted by Ian running down the stairs.

"Well? Well?" Ian asked impatiently.

Carrie stared at him blankly.

"Well, didn't you tell me you were going to be seeing Duke?" Ian asked.

"Right," Carrie agreed.

"So, you gave him my tape, right?"

Carrie's shoulders sagged with defeat. Ian's song. She hadn't mentioned it to Duke at all. She hadn't even remembered to take the tape with her. "Gee, Ian, this was a business lunch, and it really wouldn't have been the right time—"

"But you promised!" Ian cried.

"No, I really didn't promise—"

"You didn't say no!" Ian yelled. "You could have said no, but you didn't! I can't believe you did this to me!"

"Ian, I'm really sorry—"

"So what if it was business!" Ian whined. "Music is business, too!"

Carrie sighed. "Look, I can't lie to you about it, Ian. The truth is, I forgot."

"You forgot?"

Carrie nodded. "I didn't even take your tape with me. I didn't remember until you just now asked me about it."

"Gee, thanks," Ian snuffled.

"I'm really sorry," Carrie said. She ran her hand through her hair. "I feel like I've been saying that to everyone today."

"I really was counting on you," Ian mumbled, walking away with his head low.

Chloe took Carrie's hand. "Ian is mad at you, too?"

"I'm afraid so," Carrie agreed.

"Were you bad to him, too?" Chloe asked.

"I didn't mean to be," Carrie said, "but I guess I was."

Chloe nodded gravely. "You've been very bad today, Carrie. Are you going to talk to Mommy?"

Just to put the frosting on the cake? Carrie thought to herself bitterly. "I'll go talk to her now," Carrie told Chloe. "We'll try to go to a later movie." With that, Carrie turned and walked slowly toward the kitchen. She could hear, as she approached, that Claudia was still on the telephone murmuring quietly.

Carrie sat down on one of the upholstered chairs in the hallway to wait. She put her head in her hands.

I can't believe how I'm screwing everything up! Now all my friends are mad at me, my boyfriend is mad at me, Chloe is mad at me, Ian is mad at me, and I am sure Claudia is totally pissed.

Claudia's rising voice on the telephone pulled Carrie out of her thoughts.

"Wait a second, Cindi, I thought you just told me you called to apologize!"

Carrie could hear only half of the conversation. There was silence for a long moment.

"Let me get this straight," Claudia finally

said. "You called to apologize for coming out here just to hit me up for a loan, and now you're still asking me for money?"

It's Cindi Etheridge, Carrie realized. *It's got to be her.*

"It doesn't matter if you're asking for *less* money now!" Claudia exploded. "Damn right, I'm mad! I don't like being used in the name of friendship!" Carrie heard Claudia say coldly into the phone. "As far as I'm concerned, this friendship is history!"

Carrie heard Claudia hang up the phone without waiting for Cindi's reply. Then Claudia's footsteps approached the hallway.

"So," Claudia said, coming to a stop in front of Carrie and looking at her disdainfully, "is this National Take Advantage of the Templetons Week, or what?"

"I'm sorry," Carrie replied meekly.

"I bet you are," Claudia responded, her brow wrinkled with annoyance. "But not so sorry as Chloe, who has been waiting to see this movie for two days."

"I understand," Carrie said. "I fouled up. I was at lunch with Lina Weller, the filmmaker, and I got mixed up on the time I had to be back here. I really thought the movie started at quarter after three, Claudia."

"I don't care if you were having lunch with Robert Redford," Claudia shot back. "You had responsibilities here."

"That's true," Carrie said. "I made a mistake. I'm really sorry." Carrie felt near tears, but she willed them back. "I—"

"Lina Weller, who won the Academy Award for that movie about the man who was in prison for a murder he didn't commit?" Claudia interrupted.

"Uh-huh." Carrie nodded. *Is she going to get over this quickly?*

"Well, I don't care who it was," Claudia said, her tone stiffening. "You let me and my daughter down."

"I'll take her to the five o'clock show," Carrie offered.

"That's right," Claudia said. "You *will*

take her to the five o'clock show. And you are going to turn back into the responsible au pair we hired, or we're going to find someone else to do the job!"

"Fine," Carrie said, a mixture of sorrow and anger welling up inside her. "I'll go tell Chloe about the movie."

With that, she left to go find the five-year-old.

What do I need this for? Carrie thought. *I've been the best au pair I can be, and I make a couple of mistakes—no worse than Sam or Emma, that's for sure—and now the whole world wants me to eat worms. Including my best friends and my boyfriend!*

Carrie found Chloe and took her outside to play on the backyard swings before they had to go the movies. She stood in a trance, swinging the little girl for what seemed like hours, until the portable phone that was always outside rang loudly.

"I've got to get that," Carrie said to Chloe, who seemed to have completely gotten over Carrie's being late.

"Okay," Chloe said. "I'll pump. Then come back and push some more."

"You got it." Carrie grinned as she hustled over to the phone.

Why can't grownups be like kids? she thought.

"Templeton residence, Carrie Alden speaking," she answered automatically.

"Carrie!" said a slightly familiar female voice. "This is Lina Weller."

Lina Weller. Oh, my God. Why is she calling me?

"Hi, Lina," Carrie said noncommittally, though her heart was pounding a million miles an hour.

"Listen, I'm just back at the Sunset Inn with Duke. You've made quite a fan out of him."

"I have?" Carrie asked with surprise.

"Between you and me, I think his relationship with Julia you-know-who will soon be history," Lina whispered into the phone.

"Lina!" Carrie heard Duke say with annoyance in the background.

"I'm teasing you, love," Lina called to Duke. "Anyway, I really enjoyed meeting with you, Carrie. Duke tells me you are a very hard worker, that you do whatever it takes to get the job done."

Huh? Tell that to Claudia Templeton.

"Well, I try," Carrie replied.

"Carrie," Lina continued, "I'd like to offer you a position as an intern on my next film project."

"You're kidding," Carrie said with total disbelief.

"Not at all," Lina assured her. "One has to make these sorts of decisions based on gut feeling, and I got a really good feeling about you today. And what Duke had to say basically sealed it."

This is not actually happening, Carrie thought. *This is all in my imagination, and I am making it all up.*

"Oh," Carrie responded, searching for something to say.

"Oh!" Lina cried. "You must be wondering what the movie is about."

"Yes," Carrie said lamely.

"Primates. In Africa. I've met this fellow who's basically carrying on Dian Fossey's research on gorillas," Lina reported. "I've got a big grant, and TriStar is kicking in some money, too."

"Wow," Carrie said honestly. "What would I do?" *A plan was starting to take shape in her mind, a plan that had nothing to do with being an au pair on Sunset Island for Graham and Claudia Templeton, who didn't appreciate her at all.*

"Oh, it's not very glamorous," Lina said. "You'd be working for the rest of the summer in the library at Arizona State University. Doing research. Starting next week."

"Well, if I did that, would I get to go to Africa for the shoot?" Carrie asked.

"Sorry, Carrie, but that's not how it works," Lina said. "The interns are the low guys on the totem pole, so to speak. I suppose if enough funding came through . . . but I couldn't make any promises. Still, it could be a wonderful opportunity for you anyway."

"Hey, Carrie!" Chloe cried, taking Carrie's attention away from the phone. "What about me?" She sat in the swing, motionless, kicking her legs uselessly.

"Listen, Lina," Carrie said, choosing her words carefully. "Can I have until this evening to think this over?"

"Of course," Lina said. "Let me know by, say, nine tonight. No later."

"No later," Carrie breathed. "I promise. You're staying at the Sunset Inn?"

"That's right," Lina answered.

"I'll call you," Carrie said, her heart starting to race again.

"Great! I look forward to it," Lina said, and she hung up.

Carrie turned to Chloe.

"Oh, Chloe"—she sighed—"what am I going to do?"

The little girl smiled and shrugged her shoulders. "Push me in the swing," she said, "and then take me to the movies!"

* * *

"Hello, Emma?" Carrie asked timidly into the phone. "It's me, Carrie." Carrie glanced down at her watch. Eight P.M. *I've got an hour before I have to let Lina Weller know whether I'm going to be her intern. And I really don't know what to do. I hope Emma can give me some advice.*

"Hello, Carrie," Emma said with very little warmth in her voice. "Funny, we were just talking about you."

"We?" Carrie asked.

"Me and Sam," Emma said. "She's here. Hold on, I'll put her on." Carrie heard someone get up and move, and then heard Sam pick up the other extension.

"Sam, are you there?" Carrie asked.

"Uh-huh," Sam answered, sounding supremely bored.

"I just wanted to apologize again for what happened this afternoon," Carrie began. "I don't know how that could have happened, but it did."

"It sure did," Sam said flatly.

"Well, I'm sorry," Carrie responded. "I feel like a total idiot."

"We were really hurt by what you did," Emma said softly.

"I know," Carrie said miserably. "I can't even believe I did it!"

"It's just so . . . not like you!" Emma said earnestly.

"Don't you think I know that?" Carrie cried. She took a deep breath. "Listen, how pissed off is Billy?"

"Why don't you call him yourself and find out?" Sam asked.

"I'm afraid to," Carrie admitted.

"He didn't say much," Emma reported to Carrie. "But he got this icy look on his face. . . ."

"Yeah, I saw that," Carrie said with a sigh. "Oh, God, what should I do?"

"Groveling is a good first choice," Sam suggested.

"Are you guys going to be able to forgive me?"

Silence.

"Look, I'm not perfect!" Carrie cried. "I make mistakes. I've made some huge ones lately. And I'm sorry. Really sorry."

"Okay," Emma finally said.

"Sam?"

"Yeah," Sam said grudgingly.

"Thanks," Carrie said earnestly. "Can I ask your advice about something?"

"Are you sure this is the right time?" Emma asked. "I mean, it's sort of weird timing, all things considered, you know?"

"You're still mad at me!" Carrie cried.

"Hey, we can't turn our emotions on and off like faucets!" Sam exploded. "Give it a rest, okay!"

"But I really need some help with this," Carrie implored her friends. "And it can't wait, it really can't!" She quickly explained to them about Lina Weller's offer.

"Wow, first a part in a movie, then forgetting your friends, and now flying off to work with Lina Weller," Sam said. "Tough life."

"But . . . but I thought you'd be happy for me—" Carrie began.

"We are," Emma interjected.

"You don't sound like it," Carrie said miserably.

"Carrie, I know how much you like to make everything okay all the time," Emma said, "but you can't rush this."

"I guess you're right," Carrie agreed glumly. "But—" Carrie started to speak, and then stopped herself. *I know what they're talking about,* she thought. *How did I get myself into this kind of a mess?*

"Okay," Carrie said finally. "I understand. Can I call you guys tomorrow?"

"Sure," Emma said.

"I'll probably take your call," Sam said coolly.

"Okay then, see you guys," Carrie said, and hung up.

She sat there, staring at the phone. *I must be really losing it,* Carrie thought. *I just did a part in a movie and made five thousand dollars. I got to kiss Duke Under-*

wood. And Lina Weller just offered me a position as an intern on her next film. So why do I feel so awful?

She stared out the window for a long moment, lost in thought. And then, finally, she knew just what she wanted to do. Quickly Carrie looked up the number of the Sunset Inn in the phone book.

I've made my decision, she thought to herself. *What am I waiting for?* She reached down, dialed the number, and asked for Lina Weller's room when the desk clerk answered.

"Lina Weller," a polished voice answered the phone on the second ring.

"Lina," Carrie said, amazed that she was as calm as she appeared to be. "This is Carrie Alden, and I'm calling about your intern position."

TWELVE

Carrie tried not to let her hand shake as she knocked on the front door of the house Billy shared with the rest of the band members. It was the next night. After being Super Au Pair all day (she'd even called up Duke and asked him if she could drop Ian's tape by his hotel), Carrie had called and asked Billy if she could come over so they could talk. He'd said yes, but he hadn't sounded very enthusiastic about it.

Carrie had driven over to the large old house that the Flirts rented. Even as she stood there nervously waiting for Billy to answer the door, she wasn't sure what she was going to say to him.

Finally the door opened. Billy stood there in baggy jeans and a flannel shirt. Carrie didn't think she'd ever seen anyone so beautiful in her life.

"Hi," Carrie said through the screen door.

Wordlessly Billy opened the screen door and ushered Carrie into the living room. She looked around nervously. "Where is everyone?"

Billy shrugged. He sat down on the couch.

Carrie sat in an overstuffed armchair. "You're not making this easy."

"I didn't know I was supposed to," Billy said coldly.

"Look, Billy, I'm really sorry. I really messed up, okay?" Carrie said earnestly.

"No kidding," Billy said sarcastically.

"I wasn't blowing you off at all," Carrie continued. "I just . . . I got so excited about the possibility of meeting Lina Weller—I mean, she's one of my idols—that I just forgot—"

"Carrie, people don't forget about things that are really important to them," Billy said in a hard voice.

"Is that really what you think?" Carrie whispered.

Billy got up and paced around the room. "What am I supposed to think? First you're in this movie with Mr. TV Stud, and he's all over you—"

"It was in the script—" Carrie protested.

"Like I said, he's all over you," Billy continued in a grim voice, "and then you forget you have a date with me, and then you throw me out of the house, and then the next day you show up *supposedly* to meet me, but you're really there with this TV jerk again! Now, what the hell am I supposed to think, huh?"

Carrie walked over to Billy. "I swear to you, this has nothing to do with Duke. He's a friend, that's all."

Billy made a face. "How stupid do I look?"

Carrie put her hands on her hips. "Billy, do I insist that you must be hot for every cute girl who throws herself at you? I mean, you are being completely unfair here—"

"Oh, you mean he did throw himself at you!" Billy exclaimed.

"No! That's not what I meant at all!" Carrie yelled. She put her hand on her forehead wearily. This was not going well at all. "Look, can we just sit down and talk about this calmly? Please?"

Billy sat on the couch and folded his arms. Carrie sat next to him.

"Look, Billy, I admit I made some mistakes. And I've apologized for that. But I'm not involved with Duke in any way other than as a friend. The kissing was for the movie. I got paid for it, which is why I did it."

Billy nodded imperceptibly.

"The other stuff, well, I just . . . screwed up," Carrie said. "I got overextended, I guess. Somehow everything just piled up on me. I don't know how it happened. I mean, I always rag on Sam for not being responsible. . . ."

"It's just so . . . not like you," Billy mumbled.

"Emma said the exact same thing," Carrie commented. "And I know you're both right. But then I started thinking—if Sam did this no one would be very upset—she could get away with it. But since it's me, and since Carrie doesn't screw up, everyone is all over my case!"

"I guess that's true," Billy said reluctantly.

"Billy, I remember a couple of weeks ago we were supposed to meet for lunch, and you got all caught up writing some new song with Pres, and you lost track of time, and you showed up an hour late," Carrie recalled. "And another time you broke a date with me because you were so ragged out from being on the road. I've always been understanding about that, haven't I?"

"Yeah," Billy agreed.

"So why are the rules different for me than they are for you?" Carrie asked. "Because I'm a girl?"

"No, you know I'm not into that sexist crap," Billy insisted.

"Are you sure?" Carrie asked. "Because that's how it seems to me right about now."

Billy looked at her steadily. "I guess . . . I guess it threw me because . . . God, Carrie, I don't know!" Billy exploded. "Because I'm damned jealous!"

Carrie stared at him.

"You happy now?" Billy yelled.

"You don't need to take my head off—"

"I don't want to be jealous!" Billy yelled. "It's a stupid, wasted emotion, and I don't like feeling this way!"

Carrie smiled and put her hand on Billy's arm. "Billy, I get jealous, too, sometimes."

"Yeah, but that's different," Billy insisted. "You're a—"

"Girl?" Carrie finished with an arched eyebrow.

Billy stared at her. "Busted," he admitted.

"I'm glad to know you care about me that much," Carrie said. "I'd worry a whole lot more if you *never* got jealous!"

"Carrie, lemme tell you, I *hate* feeling this way," Billy said fervently.

"Then let me see if I can make you feel better," Carrie said softly. She kissed him on his forehead, his eyes, his cheeks, near his lips, and finally gave him a lingering kiss on his mouth.

"Did you do this to Duke?" Billy asked sullenly.

"Yes," Carrie whispered truthfully. "But I pretended it was you."

Then she softly said his name over and over, and kissed him until he knew she was telling him the truth.

"Wow, you showed up," Sam said sarcastically when Carrie walked into the Play Café two hours later. "Or are you here to meet someone else?"

"Holding a grudge doesn't become you," Carrie said lightly, sliding into their usual booth next to Emma.

She'd called Emma and Sam that afternoon and asked them to meet her, and they'd both agreed.

"Did you guys order yet?" Carrie asked.

"Pizza with everything," Sam reported. "Even the dainty maiden across from me has agreed to chew on some grease tonight." She took a sip from her Coke. "So, you rang?"

"Well, I just wanted us all to hang out," Carrie said. She looked at her two friends. "It feels funny, though, doesn't it?"

Emma nodded honestly. "But everything will be okay, Carrie. This isn't World War Three or anything—"

"But everything I did was just so 'not me,' " Carrie finished with a sigh. "I know."

"Hey, look who just walked into the café," Sam said, cocking her head toward the door.

Carrie turned around. It was Claudia.

"Huh," Carrie said with surprise. "She never comes in here." Carrie watched as Claudia took a seat near the door and looked at her watch. "Looks like she's meeting someone."

"I know! It must be Duke Underwood!" Sam screeched. "Whoa, baby, whatta scandal!"

"Duke is in love with Julia you-know-who," Carrie reported.

"So, how much fun was it to kiss him?" Emma asked, a twinkle in her eye.

"Fun," Carrie admitted with a small grin.

"Don't tell Billy that," Sam warned. "Tell him it was loathsome, disgusting, the most sickening moment of your young life—"

"I told him the truth," Carrie said, "which is that actually I thought about him while I was kissing Duke."

"For real?" Sam asked skeptically.

"Yep," Carrie confirmed.

"You are truly strange," Sam opined, shaking her head. "Did you and Billy make up?"

Carrie nodded and grinned. "You could say that."

"Why, you little vixen!" Sam exclaimed. "You mean everyone has forgiven you? You're totally out of the doghouse?"

"Not exactly," Carrie said, glancing again over at Claudia. "For one thing, I think I came within a hair's breath of losing my job. It's going to take some time before I'm in Claudia's good graces again."

"In other words, you have to brownnose for a while," Sam translated.

"Something like that," Carrie agreed.

"Pizza time!" Sam called out happily as Patsi, their favorite waitress, set the large pizza on the table.

"Pig out and enjoy!" Patsi said as she walked away.

"This even looks good to me tonight," Emma said, daintily pulling a slice of pizza off the pie.

"Knowing you, you'll eat it with a knife and fork," Sam teased, folding the pizza into her mouth. "Yummmm!"

"What did you decide to do about that job

with Lina Weller?" Emma asked, taking a small bite of pizza.

"Well, I did call her and I did make a decision," Carrie said. "I—" But just at that moment her attention was taken by someone coming into the café. "I don't believe it," Carrie murmured as she watched a woman come into the café and take a seat with Claudia.

"Who's that?" Emma asked, looking over at Claudia's table.

"It's Cindi, Claudia's extremely ex–best friend," Carrie explained.

As Carrie watched, Claudia and Cindi had an animated conversation over dessert and coffee, then Claudia handed Cindi what clearly looked like a check. Finally Claudia and Cindi hugged each other, and then both women left.

"Will wonders never cease," Carrie marveled.

"Are you planning to let us in on this?" Sam asked between bites of pizza.

"Well, it seems that Claudia and Cindi

were these inseparable best friends back in high school," Carrie began, and she told Emma and Sam the whole story. "So, the last I heard, Cindi had called up to try for another loan, and Claudia yelled at her and hung up on her!"

"That's terrible!" Emma cried. "Over money? Something as stupid as money?"

"It's only stupid to you because you have it," Sam pointed out to her, pulling some cheese off her pizza.

"I guess they lost touch after they both got married," Carrie said. "Cindi said she tried to stay in touch with Claudia, but after Claudia married Graham, she cut Cindi out of her life."

"That sucks," Sam said flatly. "And I want you to know that when I get Duke Underwood away from Julia you-know-who, I will still return your calls."

"Seriously, though," Carrie said thoughtfully, "I had a hard time understanding why Claudia was so angry that Cindi came to her for a loan. I mean, she was really, really ticked. She said she felt used—"

"Maybe she thought Cindi didn't care about her," Emma suggested, "and the only reason she was contacting her was because she has money."

"Yeah," Carrie agreed. "But you know, it really made me wonder. About friendships." She looked at her two best friends. "We could never just . . . lose touch with one another like that, could we?"

"Never happen," Sam assured her.

"But I bet Cindi and Claudia once said that to each other," Carrie continued. "I mean, for example, what if I'd done one more thing to tick both of you off? What if you hadn't been able to forgive me? Great friendships get thrown away over stupid stuff like that!"

"That's a scary thought," Emma said contemplatively, stirring the ice in her drink.

"So, how about if we make some kind of pact?" Sam suggested. "We won't let a stupid fight break up our friendship, and we won't let marrying some guy with money break us up, either!"

"Do you really think a pact is going to make a difference?" Carrie said sadly. "Things change. People grow apart sometimes."

"Well, I just don't buy that sob song," Sam stated firmly. "We don't have to be like that. We do have a choice, you know."

"The truth is, I can't even imagine my life without the two of you," Carrie said quietly.

"Hey, look at the bright side!" Emma suggested. "Claudia and Cindi didn't see each other for years, and they had that huge fight, and still it looked as if Claudia came through for her friend in the end."

"You know, you're right," Carrie said slowly. "Claudia must have changed her mind and called Cindi and invited her back here."

"And everyone lives happily every after," Sam sang, snagging another piece of pizza.

"But they lost each other . . . for years,"

Carrie said. "I just couldn't stand if that ever happened to us." She looked directly at Emma. "Which leads me back to the answer I gave Lina about that intern job."

"Excuse me, but that sentence didn't make any sense," Emma pointed out.

"No, I guess it didn't," Carrie agreed. "What I mean is, I don't want to ever take the two of you for granted. I didn't take the intern job because it involves research about something I don't have any interest in. Primates in Africa. I'm really not the best person for the job."

Emma's eyes lit up. Her greatest dream was to go to Africa, possibly in the Peace Corps, and to study primates.

Carrie smiled at Emma. "But you are. I recommended you instead."

Emma's mouth fell open. "You—?"

Carrie nodded.

"You did that just to prove that you don't take me for granted?" Emma said faintly.

"That was part of it," Carrie admitted.

"Hey, could you prove you don't take me

for granted by getting me a date with Duke?" Sam suggested jokingly.

Carrie laughed. "I'll have to think of something incredible for you sometime soon. The point is, I . . . I really love you guys, and I acted like an idiot, and I'm really sorry."

"Carrie, you are incredible," Emma said. "You didn't have to do anything like this to prove that you care, or to make anything up to me. You don't have to be perfect!"

"Hey, that's what I always tell you!" Sam pointed out to Emma.

"Well, it's true for Carrie, too," Emma said. Her eyes grew wide. "You really recommended me?"

"I gave her your number at the Hewitts'," Carrie said. "I hope that's okay."

"Okay? It's incredible!" Emma exclaimed.

"You know, I'm still hungry," Sam said. "How about if we order another pizza?"

"Where do you put it?" Emma marveled.

"Did you ever wish you could just stop

your life right where it is, so nothing will change, nothing bad will happen?" Carrie asked suddenly.

"Uh-oh, she's getting into one of her deep moods," Sam warned.

"I just always want the three of us to be together," Carrie said with a shrug.

"So we will, we will!" Sam cried. "Hey, let's keep in mind that it's not like we started out with anything in common in the first place!" Sam added with a laugh. "No one in the world would expect the three of us to be best friends! By the way, I promise that as long as I'm not broke I'll always loan the two of you money, you can count on it!"

They all laughed.

"I promise you can always count on me," Carrie said seriously. "In the important ways, I mean. For the long haul."

"Maybe we should, like, cut ourselves and mush our blood together and become blood sisters," Sam suggested.

"That's repulsive," Emma stated.

"I know," Sam said gleefully. "I only said it to gross you out."

Carrie looked at her friends. "I guess there really aren't any kind of guarantees, are there?" she said slowly.

"I guess not," Emma agreed sadly.

"Okay, okay," Sam agreed grudgingly. "But girlfriends, we can do our damnedest, right?"

"Right!" Carrie replied with a laugh. "And our damnedest is the very best there is!"

They clinked glasses in a toast to being best friends forever and hoped with all their hearts that their toast would always be true.

SUNSET ISLAND MAILBOX

Dear Cherie,

I am a huge fan of Sunset Island. I'd like to say that my favorite character has been Sam's buddy Danny from Sunset Secrets. I like him much better than Pres. Is there any chance of Danny returning to the island—and to Sam?

Sincerely,
Kristie Casey
Decatur, AL

Dear Kristie,

I like Danny, too! You're in luck. Danny returns in Sunset Wishes and Sunset Glitter (coming out in September and October of this year). Who do the rest of you think is a better boyfriend for Sam—Danny or Pres? Or maybe neither one? Let me know!

Best,
Cherie

Dear Cherie,

Your books are the absolute best I ever read and believe me I've read several hundred. I've read all the Sunset books, as well as Sunset After Hours and Sunset After Midnight. I want to read Sunset After Dark but everywhere I go it already sold out!

Love,
Amanda Hedleston
Culpeper, Virginia

Dear Amanda,

As you can see I took an excerpt from your letter—which was much longer and really fabulous! You have a killer imagination! You can order any Sunset book you can't find with the order form in the back of some of the Sunset Island books, or ask the book store clerk to special order it for you.

Best,
Cherie

Dear Cherie,

Hi, I really love your books. You can really relate to teens realistically. One of the biggest problems facing teens is drugs. I've seen a lot of my friends get into drugs. I think your books influence teens quite a bit. It would be a big help if you could have a book about someone getting into drugs.

Thanks,
Jennifer Salib
Grand Falls,
New Brunswick, Canada

Dear Jennifer,

You've made a really good point and I will give this a lot of thought. I've already tackled drinking and driving in *Sunset Secrets*—those of you who have read it know the dire consequences. I'd like to hear from readers on this one. Are many of the kids you know doing drugs? How is it affecting their lives?

Best,
Cherie

Dear Readers,

Okay, guys, Jeff and I just returned from the greatest vacation. We went to Hawaii for a family reunion (hi, Dad!). Jeff learned to surf from an incredibly cool woman—surfing champion Nancy Emerson. We went to watch the expert surfers on the north side of the big island, swam, snorkeled, and watched the gorgeous sunsets. We also got to hang out with our nieces—future *Sunset Island* readers Shannon, Juliet and Serena—and our hockey-crazed nephew, Chad.

Speaking of cool stuff, did I ever mention that I I get letters from literally all over the world? It is awesome! Canadian fans write a lot (keep 'em coming, eh?). I've also heard from readers in Germany, Denmark, England, Finland, and Singapore. Wow, this means Sam, Emma, and Carrie have an international rep!

Of course, I receive incredible letters from all over the United States. I got my first letter from Hawaii from Lyndsay Yee in Kailua. Congrats to Jamie Pitts of Sebring, Florida, for catching an eye-color mix-up in one book! And finally, major applause for Alison Pompora of Stamford, Connecticut, on getting your cast off!

Well, I've got to run—*Sunset Island* awaits. As always, keep on reading and I'll keep on writing. You guys are everything!

See you on the island!

Best—

Cherie Bennett

Cherie Bennett
c/o General Licensing Company
24 West 25th Street
New York, New York 10010

geartesein

CHERIE BENNETT
BELIEVERS
F A N C L U B

Hey, Readers! You asked for it, you've got it!

Join your Sunset sisters from all over the world in the greatest fan club in the world...
Cherie Bennett Believers Fan Club!

Here's what you'll get:

★ a personally-autographed-to-you 8x10 glossy photograph of your favorite writer
     (I hope!).
★ a bio that answers all those <u>weird questions</u> you always wanted to know, like how
     Jeff and I met!
★ a three-times yearly newsletter, telling you <u>everything</u> that's going on in the worlds
     of your fave books, and me!
★ a personally-autographed-by-me membership card.
★ an awesome bumper sticker; a locker magnet or mini-notepad.
★ "Sunset Sister" pen pal information that can hook you up with readers all over the
     world! Guys, too!
★ and much, much more!

So I say to you – don't delay! Fill out the request form here, clip it, and send it to the
address below, and you'll be rushed fan club information and an enrollment form!

Yes! I'm a Cherie Bennett Believer! Cherie, send me information and an
enrollment form so I can join the **CHERIE BENNETT BELIEVERS FAN CLUB!**

My Name _____

Address _____

Town _____

State/Province _____ Zip _____

Country _____

CHERIE BENNETT BELIEVERS FAN CLUB
P.O. Box 150326
Nashville, Tennessee 37215 USA

items offered may be changed without notice